LIFE

BY

DES MCANULTY

Copyright

Cover design by Mark Wilson

Editing by http://www.edit-my-book.com

Acknowledgements

Big thanks to the family, Mum, Dad, Julie, Jim and Kenny who have loved and educated me more than I could ever have wanted.

Thanks to all my mates Paul, Gerry, Iain, Maffy, Jaj, McGorry (what's the story?), Jimmy, Noel, Dom, Fr Gerard, Kenny G, The Dyle, Joe, Andy, Totten and loads more I could mention. You have inspired every word in this book and hopefully more in the future.

Thanks to Tom Sellick for his initial forensic proof read and edit

Thanks to Mark Wilson and everyone at PADDY'S DADDY PUBLISHING for their much needed guidance and support.

Thanks to Stephanie Dagg for editing the book.

Finally to my partner Kerry and wee boy Elliott. I couldn't have done this without you. For your love and patience, I am eternally grateful.

Dedication

This book is dedicated to the everlasting memory of Kevin McAnulty James Casey.

CHAPTER 1

FAR TOO MUCH TO DREAM LAST NIGHT

I SHOULD GET RID OF IT. IT WOULD BE an appropriate closure moment, as the young team are inclined to say these days. It's not like I don't know what it says. I have read this front page (along with the double spread on pages four and five) so many times that I can rhyme off its entire content from memory. *Motherwell Times* August 14th 2002. The day after Clare's body was found. To begin with I had kept the cut-outs from bigger, more prominent newspapers (*The Sun*, *Record* and *Herald* all ran with the story) but it was the *Times* issue I couldn't part with. I don't know why this was. Perhaps it was the personable nature of it: the fact that it was the local paper and it was a local event that had touched so many people. It lay beside me in my bed, night after night, as I tried to make sense of the senseless.

The warm glowing feeling that's been swimming through me for what seems like a lifetime starts to slowly subside as I grudgingly accept that the world I am in now is different from the one I have just left. In this one, she's gone. Dreams. Weird when you think about. They are supposed to represent the absolute epitome of everything we want or want to be. Dream job, dream girl, dream holiday. But has anyone ever gone to sleep and suddenly gained everything they ever wanted or wanted to be? Freud says they're the gateway to reality and if that's correct, I'm fucked. You see when I'm in the land of the living I'm fine... well, not fine exactly, but I have some degree of control at least, and can block certain unwanted thoughts. I can physically stop myself from thinking about what happened. But as soon as I hit the Big Zeds, I'm back, back with her, and she's telling me why, but I can't hear her. And it's shite, useless pointless shite, but there's nothing, absolutely nothing, I can do about it.

I have one of those annoying radio clocks that beam the time onto the ceiling, which means you have a constant reminder of your poor punctuality. It's currently telling me that it's 08:50, which means in eleven minutes' time I will officially be late for my lecture, for the third time this week. It's only Geography though, which I hate. Did it at school, hated it then, hate it even more now. Now don't get me wrong, I am under no illusions as to what this course is all about. I mean, an HND in Social Sciences will hardly get you a pint bought at the NASA Christmas party, and Motherwell College hasn't sent many Dear John letters out to the up and coming intellectual elite telling them to perhaps try Oxford. There are no prospects here. This a course designed for ex-steel worker union members, battered housewives trying to start a new life and lazy-arse chancers who don't want to work; who think being a full-time student somehow constitutes a proper career and will probably be doing something similar, somewhere similar ten years from now. And then there's me, Stevie Costello. Where do I fit in? Fucked if I know.

OK, nine o'clock now, if I get a groove on I'll make Psychology, which, incidentally, I do like. I'm showered and shaved in twenty minutes. The zipper I pull on is nearing its next Persil date, but the deodorant and aftershave of previous days manage to keep the fustiness at bay. Before I go, I take a long, self-satisfied look around my flat. It's clean, not spotlessly clean, but it's definitely well kept. I share it with a girl called Lisa who's also doing Social Sciences up at the college. She's in a different class from me though. When we moved in together, the one principle we both shared was a hatred of the preconceived notion that all students had to live like tramps. She's a wee cracker Lisa. There's nothing romantic or sexual between us and there never will be. Her spirit's always impressed me though. Always speaks her mind, always wants to help, never late for lectures, never late with essays. Aye, no doubt about it, definitely in a different class from me.

I make my way out of the flat onto the newly washed landing. The sterile smell of bleach effortlessly replacing the stagnant smell of pish. The silver steeled lift rumbles me from seventh floor to ground and I make me way out to a world called Motherwell. It's only October, yet already I can see my breath. The people I pass on the way up to the bus stop at the cross seem to revel in the hopeless limitations of their surroundings.

You see, Motherwell is different from other towns in Scotland in that it suffers from geography. It's planted firmly between Glasgow and Edinburgh. So whereas other townies in this country can get on with life because they know no different, Motherwell folk are close enough to Scotland's two main cities to be reminded of the endless possibilities and opportunities city life can offer compared to their humdrum existence. The town centre itself is a Mecca for the pound shop enthusiasts. Everywhere you look there are old women with rubber gloves, peg bags, dishcloths, shite, shite, shite. This is what comes from being routinely told by newspapers and politicians that they live in a ghost town, decimated by the closure of the Ravenscraig.

Honestly man, the way people go on about that place, like it was the only source of life we had. The truth is it was killing the folks around here. With the beer money it provided and the deadly toxins it spewed out every other night. I remember drinking carry outs down the Duchy back in the day. At nine o'clock precisely every night we'd hear a boom and the sky would light up. A blast from the 'Craig and we would drunkenly stare into the sky in wonderment at the light show provided. God knows what they there

were firing into the skies back then – but for their sake, I hope He doesn't.

When the 267 to West Crindledyke finally arrives, I hop on and put my money in the wee slot thingy. I can't help but be bowled over by the gushing charm of the bus driver. His eagerness to help and burning desire for me to have a nice day is positively overwhelming. The torn face wanker! The bus is mobbed and I struggle to find a seat. As I walk past I can hear wee snippets of conversation.

"That's the guy whose girlfriend…"

I'd heard it all before and would probably hear it again. They didn't know why Clare did what she did, neither did her friends or family and, more frustratingly, neither did I. I finally take a seat at the back next to a wee spazzy fella.

"Hiya," he slebers as I sit down.

"Oh hiya, pal, you, eh, goin up the college aye?" *Could be doing without this.*

"Uh huh, ah've goat me piece box, it's a Motherwell one, am a Motherwell fan."

"Are ye mate, aye?" I ask in mock surprise.

"Aye, ma favourite player is Faddy, but ay doesnae play for us noo, he's signed fir Scotland."

The wee man's roaring this info at me and people are beginning to look round, but which freak they're looking at isn't exactly clear. Once the arduous bus journey comes to a thankful end, I make my way up Dalziel Road. The college sits in the middle of a forested area and all paths leading to it are awash with brown sludgy leaves that stick to your trainers. It's also directly adjacent to the main Catholic school in this area and I get some brave sideways abuse from a couple of greasy purple-blazered teenagers. I try my best to ignore them and eventually turn left into the big grey building, which clearly doesn't fit in with its more serene surroundings. A familiar sense of foreboding slowly starts to creep through me as I climb the stairs to the lecture room. I don't like this place; in fact, I hate it.

Carolyn Moran is the head of the Social Sciences department and specializes in Psychology. Although a class-A nippy sweetie, she can at least teach and she seems to like me. This was partly due to the fact that most of the stuff I hand in is of merit standard, but also because she's, well, a woman. And women have always liked me. Sounds horrible I know, but it's true. The problem with me is I've never had the confidence to exploit it.

"Let us consider shall we, the result of an experiment that contains a scale attenuation problem. Scarborough was interested in the question of modality differences in retention. Do we remember information better when it's presented to the eyes and ears simultaneously, or to one or the other?"

Carolyn scans the class to see if they're taking notes, which most of them furiously are. I look around and

try to figure out what I'm doing here. Again it sounds big-headed, but I'm better than this. I mean these are genuinely good people and, despite the predictability of their backgrounds, I do admire them for not accepting the status quo and trying to make a better life for themselves. But I want to be at University doing this. Not for the exaggerated wackiness of the lifestyle (God forbid) but for the stimulus. I mean I enjoy subjects like Psychology, but I just wish I was doing it at a more challenging level.

It's my fault, I suppose. I wasted my last two years at school and totally blew my exams. My old man decided that he could give me everything his money could buy, apart from a stable family life. He fucked off to Australia with his girlfriend Mandy, leaving me with my Aunty May and Uncle John, who, for two years, tried to bring up a kid that was nearing the end of the bringing-up stage and had a massive chip on his shoulder. Mum had left me and my dad seven years earlier, but that, as they say, is another story.

At lunch break, I head for the canteen. I have a wee look to see if I can see Lisa, but she's not about. The place is full to the rafters. The wee schemie neds from the mechanic YTS courses *or whatever they're called now* are glaring menacingly at anyone who goes by. I don't get these kids. They are ritually ridiculed daily by the newspapers. They're ripped to shreds by comedy programmes and comedians. Papers they read, programmes they watch, yet they continue to play the stereotype while they fast become the lepers of the twenty-first century.

I decide to go outside for some fresh air where I'm met by big George and Andy, two ex 'Craig men who are in my class. I find them pleasant enough, but get the impression that Andy clings to George a bit too much. George is a no-nonsense type of guy, but intelligent with it, whereas Andy struggles with the course work. I can remember coming down on enrolment day. I sat next to them both as we filled in the necessary paperwork. Andy looked like a rabbit in the headlights as the form fired relentless, hard hitting questions like "Date. Of. Birth." In the end, big George filled the thing in for him. I have the feeling George had been doing the same thing in the twenty years they endured in the steelworks.

I'm just about to crack on with my sandwich, when Andy starts babbling on about the amount of course work Carolyn has assigned him to do compared to the other lecturers.

"Ah mean, ah've goat the weans, Stevie, and she works," he says incredulously.

"Aye," George laughs. "An the Champions league, fishing on a Saturday and yer wee games a pool on a Sunday afternoon up the Club." He says this whilst winking in my direction, making me feel like a video-cop from a seventies police drama.

Just as Andy's about to argue his case, a lecturer who's around the same age as George and Andy and teaches on the fourth floor, walks towards us. She's in her forties and wears an all-in-one business suit

that suitably sets off her impressive figure. She walks with a slight swagger, which exudes a sexiness that helps to disguise the impending ageing process visible around her eyes and neck. As she passes, she looks towards me, flicks her dyed red fringe, catches my gaze and holds it for a second in that slightly slutty way single woman of her age are prone to do.

"Here, did ye see that, did ye Stevie, did ye see it? Gave ye the wee look there, ma son!" Andy says excitedly, swinging his hips Tom Jones style. "Big thing ay, would ye George, would ye?"

I don't know why she did it, or if she meant it. I've noticed girls looking at me before. And lately everyone's been staring at me because of Clare. I've never been that good with girls though. I can never work out what they want from me. My big mate Stubbsy's a natural. Any time we're out and about I'll catch some girl looking in my direction. But once the chat kicks in, it's the boy Stubbs they go for every time.

We get an extended lunch break thanks to the continuing absence of our Literature lecturer, Mary, and her dodgy bowel system. It's one of those cloudy but mild days. I decide to have some time on my own and head up to the embankment that overlooks the Special Needs building. I sit on the dry grass, look down on the wheelchair ramp and let my mind wander back to a time when things were less complicated.

Clare. It was here that we first met. I was running an errand for Carolyn; taking a folder of paperwork to a Learning Difficulties teacher in the building. As I walked up the stairs and made my way through the doors, I caught a carer struggling to push a wheelchair up the ramp. She didn't particularly stand out right away. Brown, curly hair that I later found out was natural, big brown eyes, little to no make-up, baggy blue jeans and T-shirt. Very understated. Despite not being drawn initially by her looks, I was immediately impressed with the way she went about her job. Although she was struggling with the strain of the wheelchair, she continued to make light jokes with the kid sitting in it; blowing the hair from her face, determined to reach their intended destination. I hurriedly ran down the ramp and began to push one handle as she manoeuvred the other.

"Thank you," she beamed as we eased the chair through the double doors.

"Aye, nae bother."

"Haven't seen you up here before? Seen you down the main building, right enough," she said hesitantly.

"Stevie," I said, offering my hand.

"Clare. What you studying?"

"Social Sciences," I said almost apologetically.

"Oh, you like your politics then?"

"Eh aye, we do political theory, ah enjoy it actually." I was slightly puzzled at this random inquiry.

"Well ah hope you'll be joining us down the library on Thursday, Dad's always keen to spread the word to new disciples," she laughed, pointing to a flyer on the notice board. It was for a question and answer session with Jack Murray, MSP for Motherwell and Wishaw, left-wing fly in the ointment for the Scottish Labour Party, and a genuine hero of mine.

Jack had been a member of the Labour Party all his days. He was old school in the vein of Benn and Skinner, yet was fundamental in selling the New Labour model to an unconvinced Scottish electorate. He was chosen as the candidate for the new Scottish Parliament after being cruelly overlooked by then Scottish Secretary Helen Liddell for the Westminster post, in favour of one of her own lapdogs, Frank Roy. He won by a leg and a country mile.

I don't know if it was the revelation of who her dad was, but I instantly became attracted to Clare and after that I did indeed go see her father at the library. He was brilliant. Electrifying. The way he could passionately put across the argument for the totalitarian re-distribution of the country's wealth, yet somehow convince the audience it could be delivered by a left of centre (who were more centre than left) Labour administration was something to behold. I sat next to Clare. She had made more of an effort with her appearance. She sat quietly through the speech showing little emotion. She didn't seem nervous for her dad during it or proud of him afterwards, which I found to be a little strange. I contended that this was due to sheer over-exposure.

Impressive as it was for me, she had been listening to this speech since she was a little girl.

I asked her to come to the pub and she breezily accepted. The ease with which she could make decisions on a whim, seemingly without fear of consequence, seemed to draw me to her more.

We went to this place not far from the library, the Railway Tavern. We managed to talk for ages about everything and nothing without pausing for awkwardness to take over. She spoke little of her father, which was a wee bit disappointing. Instead, she told me all about her dreams of New York, clothing labels, settling down in remote Scottish Islands, and big, big families. She was something fresh and new to me and for the next seven months we were inseparable. Clare Murray, woman of my dreams, tormentor of my nightmares.

The afternoon kicks off with History, just the same old Standard Grade crap. The lecturer, Ted Mullen, a wee round guy who always wears the same grey suit that smells of homemade soup, is telling us how Hitler reached out to the German electorate by promising work and wealth to the left-wingers of the country, and European dominance to appease the right. Which is fair enough, I suppose, but I don't buy into the notion that the whole of Germany was behind him. I mean, a lot of them, farmers, tradesmen and the like, probably took nothing to do with the Third Reich and only wanted to get on with their lives. A Jewish schola, can't remember his name, once said that all roads to Nuremberg were awash with apathy, which I think was probably right. Most of the Germans were probably unaware what that nutter was really up to.

After class, I make my way down the town to meet Big Stubbsy for a pint, spending more money I don't have. Dad sends cash over for me, but it's never enough, or rather I never make it enough. I went for a job interview the other day up at Safeway Wishaw, or Morrisons, as it's known now. It went ok, I reckon. The guy doing the interview seemed all right, even if he gave the impression of being a bit too enthusiastic about his job, a common trait in the cut-throat retail industry.

I see Stubbsy waiting for me outside the brand new discotheque, which has been cleverly designed to look like a bingo hall, making the eventual change-over as painless as possible. The big man's got a cheeky look on his face and is trying to get my attention. It doesn't take me long to find out why. A wee Asian babe has just walked past and he's obviously impressed.

"Fuckin hell, did ye see that?" he gasps. "Allah wept! You awrite, son?"

"Aye, fine mate, listen, wee Lisa's gonnae come doon and meet us if that's ok?"

"Aye, as long as she cheers herself up a bit. Tried tae speak to her last week, near bit ma fuckin heid aff."

Stubbsy and Lisa have a strange relationship. On the face of it they don't get on very well, fighting and arguing all the time, which can be a bit of a drag. But they always meet up, even when I'm not there, and when I am there it never feels uncomfortable. There are times when they have these daft, pointless rows. Yet I'm never ill at ease when the three of us are together. It's weird really.

I check my phone; there's a voicemail and it's from the Morrisons dude, gleefully telling me I have been successful in my application for the post of Replenishment Assistant. It's the guy that interviewed me and the excitement in his voice is slightly unnerving.

"Got that job, the one up Safew– sorry, Morrisons," I tell Stubbs.

"Aye? Brilliant mate, what a result, Safeway in Wishaw, you've made it son! Top ay the fuckin world," he says sarcastically. We look at each other and sing in unison, "EVERYTHING YOU WANT FROM A STORE AND A LITTLE BIT MO-O-ORE!" As we do this the big man sticks his arse out and taps his back pocket, grinning from ear to ear, not realising he's mistaking the Asda ad with the old Safeway number, the daft prick.

CHAPTER 2

WIVES, LIVES AND SUPERMARKETS

ALASTAIR BLANEY SLOWLY SCANNED THE STOCK check sheets for a third time. Produce? Bang on. Wines and spirits? A few queries, but none he could put down to human error. Daily replens? Fucking nightmare. The performance levels of the three areas of the supermarket that came under his supervision had remained fairly consistent throughout the year. They also provided Alastair with all the evidence he needed about the state of the British work ethic in this day and age.

There were those, Alastair reflected, who lived to work. They took the same pride in their work as they did their appearance. They showed the same loyalty to their colleagues as they did their football team. More importantly, they loved their workmates as much as they did their own family. On the other side of the coin there were those who despised such attitudes and hated anybody who held them dear. They sneered at any real structured work ethos, mocked those who tried to get on in life and camouflaged their laziness and commie beliefs with a hollow rebellious attitude, which they pathetically believed was one in the eye to 'The Man'. And then there were those, who, quite frankly couldn't give a toss either way.

Alastair was definitely one of the former. He had worked in Safeway Wishaw since he was sixteen. He hadn't worked anywhere else. He loved it. It was who he was. If he worked in an office as an accountant or a hospital as a doctor he would be exactly the same. He knew only too well that people made fun of him behind his back and that the more he dedicated himself to his work, the less frequently his old friends tried to get in touch. He didn't care. He was only interested in running a tight ship and turning Morrisons Wishaw into the most desirable shopping experience in Lanarkshire. His rapid rise through the ranks saw him being named Assistant Manager at the age of twenty-six, the youngest to hold such a post in Scotland. This thrilled him immensely and he vowed to take the next step up as soon as his manager, Mr Reynolds, finally got round to retiring.

Despite his inner drive to succeed, Alastair wasn't interested in the material wealth that came along with such a position. He wasn't interested in trampling all over those below him to earn a few more pounds. Although possessing the working attitude of a hardnosed capitalist, he always fought the corner of the people he thought were integral to the store's success: the staff. While they perfected unforgiving impersonations and named certain situations after him – working the weekend on top of your normal hours was known as "doing an Alastair" – they were oblivious to the fact that he had fought tooth and nail to give them the chance of overtime in the first place, with Mr Reynolds preferring to hire more part-time staff. It was also he who stood up for them when it was proposed that any task that was started before finishing time must be completed, even if it meant staying on with that bit extra unpaid. Alastair thought this was grossly unfair and disastrous for morale, so he told Mr Reynolds in no uncertain terms that he was dead against it. He knew this irritated the old man, but Alastair didn't particularly care what he thought, or what the employees he was fighting for thought of him, so he didn't go shouting it from the rooftops. He only cared about the job and getting it done to the best to his ability.

Unfortunately for Alastair, the upward trajectory of his career was in sharp contrast to the state of play at home. His marriage to his childhood sweetheart, Marie, was going through what he thought was nothing more than a difficult phase. They started going out when they both turned eighteen. She worked part time in Safeway, as it was known then, whilst studying at St Andrew's teaching college. Their blossoming romance caused a minor scandal at the time. Nothing to do with age, religion or infidelity on either part. The infamy of their relationship stemmed from the fact that Marie had actually looked in Alastair's direction in the first place. Marie was Hollywood, a class-A stunner of the first degree. One night she left the Cleland Club with the bold Alastair in tow. The workies were called in the next day to repair the jaw damage to the floor. And this, Alastair reckoned, was the fundamental problem with their relationship as far as he could see.

Ever since that night in the Cleland Club, he was constantly being told how lucky he was to be going out with Marie O'Dermott and he hated it. That's not to say he didn't know how lucky he was to be going out with someone as beautiful as Marie. She was a rare breed, with a mixture of Italian good looks that she got from her mother, and the sharp, dry sense of humour she inherited from her Irish father. If Alastair was being honest, he wasn't actually sure what it was that Marie saw in him. He knew she loved him because she never tired of telling him. But physically, with his thinnish frame and totally unremarkable features, he couldn't help but think they were somewhat of a mismatch and the more people reminded him of his good favour to be married to such a girl, the more uncomfortable about his own appearance he became.

Their problems of late were, as is the case in lots of marriages, of a sexual nature. Alastair wasn't the most sexual person in the world and could never understand, even during their pubescent age, the frenzy and desperation with which his friends discussed the opposite sex. And now, as a married man, he couldn't understand his wife's desperate need for more passion, as she put it. The truth was, despite loving his wife very much, he just wasn't a sexually passionate man and he wished Marie would understand this. He loved her, he really did. When he came home from work after a hard shift, he would sit and listen to her stories from the classroom that day. Of how she passed on to the kids something she was taught when she was a child and how the kids responded. He genuinely loved her for the person she was, but dreaded that time at night, lying in bed, when she would lean over, softly kiss his neck, teasingly smile and rub her long, smooth legs against his crotch. He wanted to sleep, to be prepared for the next day, for the rigours of running a fast-paced supermarket.

"Not tonight, hen," he would say and she would roll over, angry and frustrated.

That had been the scenario last night. Alastair had told her that he had to get up early; he was due in the disciplinary room at nine o'clock with two guys from the nightshift who had been caught on security cameras stashing out-of-date lager behind the skips, no doubt coming back for it later on.

"Well I hope you're harder in there than you are in here," Marie snapped, rolling onto her side.

In all the time he had known his wife, Alastair had never heard her say anything like that. She never made fun of him the way the others did; in fact, he was convinced she had spent the best part of the last eight years standing up for him when snidey remarks about their apparent mismatch were made, whether behind his back or to his face (or on the way out of the disciplinary room more often than not) but he could handle it. He worked hard, he was never knowingly unfair to anyone and, ever since he could remember, he had never rejected anyone's plea for help – if they couldn't see that it was their problem. With Marie, though, it was different. She was the only person, apart from his parents, who genuinely appreciated him for who he was. When he confided in her about his unpopularity, she would angrily tell him to ignore them, that she admired him and that it didn't matter what those idiots thought, it was what she thought that mattered. Yet last night she had made a dig, and it hurt.

Tonight he would make it up to her. He was supposed to be working a split shift, which usually meant him starting at nine, finishing at three, starting back at six and not finishing until the early hours of the morning. This evening, however, thanks to the relatively good results of the stocktake, he was able to knock off early. His plan was to get the most expensive bottle of wine the shop had to offer, stop for some Chinese and spend some quality time with his wife. He would try and have sex with her, be passionate with her, make her feel wanted and desired. He wished his sexual urges towards his wife were stronger, but if they were would he be the person he was now? Could he be as good at his job if he was as impassioned with the opposite sex? The thought terrified him.

He did have occasional sexual urges, but the problem was that they were rarely brought on by his wife. In fact, if he was being honest, the only girl he had ever lusted after was a nineteen-year-old called Tracy who worked in the bakery section. This was a mystery to Alastair. Tracy was by far and away the most unremarkable girl in the shop yet for some reason she had him dry of mouth and hard of cock anytime she came near him.

On one occasion, during what was just another sex session with Marie, a vision of Tracy – in all the splendour of her company-provided uniform – popped into his head. Alastair proceeded to give his wife the shortest, hardest and definitely most satisfying seeing to that she had ever had. Although feeling slightly creepy about the idea, he might delve into his unhealthy portfolio of Tracy images tonight if it would inadvertently keep his wife happy.

It was wet outside as Alastair approached his relatively new Lexus. As the slick motor silently exited the car park, he pressed the play button on the in-car stereo that was thoughtfully placed on the indicator sticks. The sound that emanated from the speakers was not of Alastair's choosing. It was a local band whose flute player taught once a week at Marie's school. It wasn't really Alastair's thing, a bit too indie, but he had to admit, the girl who was singing had a beautifully haunting voice. He decided it was too late for food and headed straight home.

The thought of a romantic night with his wife, or even a filthy one with Tracy, could not distract him from the tricky decision that had cropped up that day. He had been interviewing for the part-time posts in the produce department. The applicants sent from the job centre were, as usual, useless. In fact, they were all pretty poor, except one. He was a student at Motherwell College. He was bright, confident and, as the excitement at the checkouts would verify, a good looking kid to boot. But Alastair had read the newspapers and watched the news; he recognised him straight away. The boy had baggage.

His name was Stevie Costello and, to be fair, he openly disclosed the recent events that had taken place in his life. His girlfriend had recently committed suicide. She had been missing for weeks and her car and a note were found at the Leadhills viaduct, a notorious suicide spot. The reason it was so publicised was the girl's father. Jack Murray was the local MSP for the area. He had just been appointed Finance Minister, which excited those within the party who believed that the days of someone with leanings as left wing as Jack Murray holding such a high profile job in government were long gone. Alastair knew that employing someone who had come through such a huge and public trauma was a risk and he resolved to give the matter his full attention over the weekend.

He made his way through the quiet 'Twenty's Plenty' side streets, and manoeuvred his car into the plush new estate on the outskirts of Cleland. The first thing he noticed was that the living room light was still on in the four-bedroom town house he called home.

"Good," he thought, "she's still up."

As he swerved into the drive, something caught his eye and made him jump. Coming out of the front door was a big guy, about six feet tall. He had blond hair and seemed to quicken his step when he saw the car. Alastair's first thought was that he was a burglar and was out of the car like a shot, despite his heart beating at about ten times the normal rate.

"Who the fuck are you?" Alastair shouted, finally finding his voice. It was then that Alastair noticed that the guy, with his expensive shoes and jeans topped with a blue Fred Perry T-shirt, had a look that was more suited to a seasoned clubber than some scally on the rob. He then looked up and saw Marie standing at the door. She was also dressed up to the nines. She looked at him for a few painful seconds, then slowly walked back into the house. Alastair didn't know what was going on, but knew he didn't like it. He didn't like it one little bit.

CHAPTER 3

GENES INC.

IT'S FRIDAY THE SIXTH OF OCTOBER AND A potential disaster on the back of the 240 to Coltness has thankfully been averted. Three wide-eyed innocents are sat at the back of the bus, McDonald's straws in mouth. The paper that's used to wrap the straws has been strategically bitten off and carefully rolled by skilful mouths into neat, but deadly, pieces of ammo. The only problem is that they've got no target to hit, no bulls-eye to aim for. Luckily, my newly washed, Pantene Pro-V Plus hair has come into range. The wee bastards! I hate travelling on buses. Cannae wait to get my licence. Stevie offered me a lift. He's started working up that Safeway in Wishaw which is right next to my mam's, but I needed some time on my own to get my thoughts together.

I've only started seeing my mam again after last year's revelations and, to be honest, I'm still a bit raw about it. I don't feel comfortable in her house, ma house, the house I grew up in. I get the impression my mam feels the same. My mam, by the way, who's actually my gran.

Fuckin Sociology, what was that all about? Jean asked Tony the lecturer for the notes from Tuesday's class. She missed it because her wee ones were no keeping too well and got sent home from the school. Tony just turns to her and says, in his very own patronising way, "If I was to repeat every lecture that people couldn't be bothered turning up for, I doubt very much we would get through the course work." That's what he said, the cheeky prick. Jean was mortified to the extent that I thought she was going to burst into tears. She's really nice as well, Jean, wouldn't harm a fly. Later on, I gave her my notes from Tuesday to copy. I told her that Tony was a wanker and that she shouldn't let him get to her, which I think she appreciated.

I don't really like Sociology and that's not because of Tony. I just don't seem to get the coursework the same way I do History and Psychology. Stevie says that Sociology is the most pointless subject on the course. He says that in a country so driven by the free-market there is no room for a qualification in a subject that, at its core, champions a more coercive redistribution of the nation's wealth. Thatcher destroyed society, he says, so why the need to study it? I wish Stevie was in my class. Don't get me wrong, he always helps me when he can, but for some reason he thinks I'm some sort of super-brain. He's always telling me I can do this course – no problem – and when I get him to proofread my essays he thinks am coasting it.

"Relax, hen. Honestly, there's not a thing wrong with that. It's a strong pass, maybe even a merit." Which is easy for him to say, Mister Merit-for-the-Fuckin-Lot, thank you very much! He's a smart one all right and I'm not the only one who wants Stevie in our class. Apparently, I'm the envy of the full college because I live with sex demigod Stevie Costello. Actually, that sounds really bitchy. It's not his fault he's good looking and, to be fair, he doesn't flaunt it. Though I think this is more to do with his hatred of people who'd do such a thing, rather than any lack of knowledge of the fact. I hate all the silly innuendo every time he comes into view. I'm seen as some sort of freak because I am not sneaking into his room every night and screwing his brains out. The truth is, ever since I've known him I've never looked at him that way. And besides, when we first met he was well into Clare and, oh God I don't even want to talk about that.

"Mam." I still call her that. I know she's technically my gran, but that's what I've always called her. Kids that find out they're adopted don't start calling their parents by their first names all of a sudden.

"Hiya hen, ye had yer dinner yet?" I hadn't, but I didn't want to tell her. I was here to let her know my plans and then hopefully leave as soon as.

"No am awrite, Mam."

"How's your college goin'? We never see ye hen, ah wish we seen more of ye."

Can ye believe that? She wants to see more of me? It's like nothing's changed with her. Like we can go back to the way things were, forget the lies and deceit and go on the way things were. No way, how could I? Mental.

"Mam, ahm thinking about looking for my dad. My real dad." She looks at me with those eyes that make me feel like she's disappointed with me, like it's somehow my fault, like I have done something wrong.

"You had a father, a real father, and all this talk would have broken his heart. We're still your family Lisa, this is still your home."

This conversation has been on repeat ever since I found out exactly who I was. Almost a year now. A year since our Angela came up from Doncaster and told me over a bottle of rosy in Weatherspoons that she was my mam. Imagine someone telling you that your whole existence has been a complete falsehood. That the people who you love more than any other, the people who guide and protect you through the good and the bad, aren't who they say they are? Then imagine hearing this in fuckin Weatherspoons. Horrible. I haven't spoken to Angela again yet, but I have found out since that my dad was an apprentice down at the Ravenscraig when it was open. His family apparently moved to Dumfries to get away from the scandal and the police, since Angela was under-age.

"Ah've found where he lives, Mam, so I'd rather you accepted what ah was doing than have another falling out over this."

"A louse! That's what he was. Nothing more. Got our Angela pregnant then ran off without a care in the world. It was us, your father and me, who had to deal with it. We done what we thought was right, right for you, right for Angela, right for everybody. I know your feelin' lousy aboot whit's happened with yer pal's wee girlfriend, but this insnae goin' tae make things better, love."

I knew this would happen. She turns on the waterworks and tries to get me to change my mind.

"Ah can't talk to you when you are like this, Mam; am going outside for some fresh air."

I storm out the back door, with her still whimpering in the living room. I know that her and Dad – up until he died five years ago – had done all they could for me. It must have been hard. I start thinking about Stevie. What that boy has been through. Abandoned by his mother and, to a lesser extent, his father, and having to deal with this Clare situation. He'd probably kill to have a woman like my mother in his life. The thought makes a small lump rise in my throat. I decide there and then that if I am going to go ahead with the search for my dad, it would better to do it with Mam's blessing.

"Mam, listen," I say as I re-enter the kitchen, "ah don't want to fight over this, but it's something ah feel ah need to do and ah would rather do it with your blessing. Ah mean, come on Mam; you must have known this was going to happen sooner rather than later?"

She nods away and mentions something about my father.

I try to lighten the conversation by asking if she was heading up to the bingo. It seems to do the trick and she starts telling me about Agnes Mulholland and how she won six hundred pounds last Thursday. We sit like this for a bit and drink some tea. I tell her about my course and she listens with as much enthusiasm as she can muster. She asks after Stevie and calls him all the "poor laddies" under the sun after what happened with Clare. I promise to keep an eye on him, which I think makes us both feel better. I make my excuses to leave and promise to come up on Sunday for my tea. I walk down to the main street and start to feel better, like somehow a weight has been lifted from my shoulders. As I'm waiting for the 267 I feel my phone vibrating in my bag.

"Hello?"

"Hey missus, whit's happenin?" It's Stevie and he's in the pub by the sound of it.

"Och, not much just up seein' my mam. Where are ye?"

"Doon the Tav wi' big Stubbs, ye comin' doon?"

Although sitting with that big ignoramus is the last thing I need, I could murder a Southern Comfort.

The bus isn't long in coming and it's a better journey back, fewer people, and that unpleasant sense of foreboding has lifted. You always feel better when you've got something out the way that you've been putting off for a long time. The Tav is mobbed. Friday teatime and it's packed out. A wee goldmine this place, no doubt. I spot Stevie and Stubbs in one of the wee cosies next to the jukie. Stubbsy goes up to the bar and, as I get closer to him, he spins me round towards the ladies toilets where two teachery types are sharing a bottle of wine.

"See that one on the left? The one with the long black hair? She's been giving me the glad eye all night. Watch me go, baby, watch me go!" Usually, I would've been seething at such a comment, but tonight I ignore it. I take a seat next to Stevie and he gives me a wee peck on the cheek.

"You ok kid?" he says as Stubbsy takes his seat.

"Aye, honey, am fine," And as I take a sip of my Southern Comfort and ginger ale and let it slowly warm me up inside, for the first time in ages, I actually mean it.

CHAPTER 4

BEER FESTIVALS IN MOTHERWELL (AND OTHER GREAT IDEAS THROUGH HISTORY)

AM READY BEFORE THE BOYS! CAN YOU BELIEVE THAT? It usually takes me hours. It's part of the night, intit? I normally pour myself a wee Blossy Hill after I've washed ma hair. I light some candles, put on the chill out CD Stevie made for me and do my make-up as carefully as I can. That's what I usually do, but not tonight. I overheard Stevie inviting Stubbsy and Eddie for a drink before we go out and I thought, 'No way'. I know what would happen. I'd be in my room running about daft, trying different outfits on, while they'd be like, "Aw Lisa, c'mon tae fuck hen, that's the taxi phoned". So I thought, "Not tonight, I'll be ready waiting for them for a change." Stevie's not long after me. He comes through to the living room dressed as he always is: ripped jeans, trainers and zipper top with a T-shirt that says, 'MC5'. Whatever that means.

"Lookin' the business the night, sweetheart, like Jackie Kennedy in the eyes of my father, nae doubt."

He always says things like that to me. I love Stevie, but it's more like a brother, if you know what I mean. I can hear someone coming in. It'll be Stubbsy. He's the only one who never knocks. He swaggers past me and I catch myself flicking my hair and fixing my top. Just when I think he's getting the wrong idea, he looks at me for a second, then moves towards the kitchen without even saying a hello, the ignorant fuckin cretin! Eddie comes through and takes a seat in the living room with me.

"Hi Eddie, lookin' forward to tonight?"

"Eh aye, few beers in that."

That's all I get out of him; he's quite shy Eddie, especially with girls. He eventually gets up and walks into the kitchen to see what's keeping Stubbsy who's on the phone to someone.

I content myself with this week's edition of *Hello!* magazine. It's the usual celeb wedding crap, but I like to see what everyone's wearing. I am reading an article about Jordan and Peter Andre. It's a big double-page spread and there's a picture of her wee boy, the one that's handicapped, the poor wee soul. I am about to turn the page when Stubbsy comes up from behind me and says something that makes my fucking blood boil. Pointing at the picture of Jordon's wee boy he says, "See that, ah'd have that put doon."

I struggle for a second to try and register just what he has said, and then I just lose it.

"YOU'RE SICK, A SICK, PATHETIC BASTARD, THAT'S A HORRIBLE THING TO SAY!"

Then he tries to justify himself to Eddie and Stevie who have come in to see what all the commotion is.

"Naw man, seriously it goes for people, bites them and that." The way he says it, it's like the wee boy isnae even human.

"Right Stubbsy, that's enough," Stevie says trying to keep the peace. But no, Stubbsy has to have the last word. He puts his bottle to his mouth like it's a microphone and starts doing an impression of that Motson football commentator.

"Of course, because of the dual nationality of both his parents the lad is eligible for both England, and Trinidad and Tobago, but to be honest with you Gary, ah can't see it happening." I just get up and head for my room, drawing Stevie and Eddie the dirtiest of looks as they try to hold their laughs in.

Stevie comes through to see me. "Hey c'mon, Lisa, he's only having a laugh, you know what he's like," he says putting his arm around my shoulder.

"He hates me Stevie. That rant, it wasn't for your benefit, he said it to annoy me. Why he does it ah'll never know," I say, wiping wee tears from my eyes.

"He doesn't hate you Lisa, he's under a bit of pressure just now. Listen there's something I have to tell you. Now don't go mad, right?"

"What is it?" I say, slightly startled.

"Promise you won't go mad?"

"Promise!"

"You know when you went down to that hen weekend in Brighton a few weeks back?"

"Lesley's do? Yeah, what about it?"

"Well ehm, you eh, had a wee accident before you left."

"Accident? What do you mean, Stevie?"

"Well, ahm not sure exactly what you done, but when ah got in that night the bathroom and hall was absolutely flooded and the tap was still running."

"WHAT? Oh Stevie, you're jokin. Ah was runnin around like a mad wuman that day. Ah must not have turned the tap after brushing my teeth. Oh Stevie, am so sorry. What did you do?"

"Fuckin panicked an called you all the daft bitches under the sun. Ah phoned the letting agency and they said we had to pay for it. Well, this is like a week after the funeral and ah was like, fuck, what next, but that's when Stubbsy came in."

"What did he do?" I said as apologetically as I could.

"He told me to pack a bag and go round to his mam's and stay there for a couple of nights, said he would sort it. And he did. Came back and he had gutted and re-floored with the exact same flooring; you would never think anything had happened."

"And how did you pay for it Stevie, why did you not tell me?" I asked, absolutely incredulous now.

"Well, that's the thing. He told me a guy from one of the jobs he was on owed him a favour and done it for nothing. Ah was too pleased to even think there was something not quite right about that. It wasn't until wee Eddie came over to see me that ah found out the truth. Aye, some guy from his work came over and did the job, but ay charged him the full whack. On top of that, Stubbs went down and bought the flooring in B&Q out of his own pocket. When Eddie questioned the extent of his generosity, the big man got quite irate with him. Said that what with Clare's funeral and you and your mam and that, we had enough on our plate. He made Eddie swear not to say anything. Lisa, he's been working seven days a week to pay for it. So try and give him a break."

I try to take in what Stevie's told me. If it's true, and I've no reason to doubt him, it was an amazing gesture, but, for some reason, not surprising. Stubbsy's loyalty to his friends has never been in question. I just couldn't work out why he had so much antagonism towards me.

"God, Stevie, ah don't know what to say."

"Say, nothing, that's what he wants. Now c'mon, wipe that snot from your face and let's get going," he says lifting me from my bed.

I tidy myself up and go back into the living room where Stubbsy is again holding court as if nothing has happened. This time he's taking the piss out of Stevie. We're going to the Beer Festival up the Civic and Stubbsy is regaling a story from last year's event. A story, by the way, that me, Eddie, Stevie and even Stubbsy himself know to be a complete fabrication.

"Belgian it was, totally rank rotten man, but – obviously cause it's the strongest on the menu and this being Motherwell – the full hall's knockin it back. We just want ay git pished. But this cunt," he says, pointing towards Stevie, who's shaking his head, knowing full well what's about to be said will not put him in good light, truth or not, "he starts swirling the bottle like it's a three-hundred-year-old wine, stares into space and goes 'you know something Gary, this beer, judging by its popularity, could very well turn out to be the Super Lager for the iPod generation'."

We all fall about laughing, including Stevie and, I must admit, I feel my mood lift.

The taxi drops us off outside the front door of the old eighties style Civic Hall. We move forward to pay the entrance fee and collect our wristbands. As I reach for my purse in my bag I hear a big booming voice. "STUBBSY BOOOY!" We all look round to see a massive bouncer motioning us away from the pay area and through to the main hall.

"In ye go big fella, nae bother for you, big man," he says, despite being nearly a foot taller than Stubbs. He's a giant. Eddie is all chuffed, a wee swagger forming as he walks into the hall. Stubbsy looks nonplussed and never even looks at the doorman who lets us through. Stevie's face is like thunder.

"What's wrong with you?" I ask.

"That fuckin bouncer cunt. That's him that battered that lassie over at Hamilton Palace." I think for a minute, then I remember. A poor couple were over having a few drinks in the Palace. A bouncer told them to move out of the piano bar. They said they would once they finished their drinks. Am not actually sure what happened, but an argument ensued and two bouncers held the boyfriend and made him watch as that big monster kicked lumps out of his girlfriend. It must have been terrible for both of them.

"C'mon," I say to Stevie, linking his arms, "Ah'll get you one of your favourite iPod beers, haha."

"Fuck off, you," he laughs, burying his head into my shoulder.

The night goes ok after that. I try as many of the lighter beers as I can, before feeling bloated and going to pee for the fifth time. Eventually, I ask Eddie to get me a white wine. The place is getting louder and louder and I notice Stevie grimacing at the local band that is playing the usual local indie music up on the stage. Eddie and Stubbs seem to be having a competition to see who can drink the most of the beers at the stronger end of the menu. I'm sipping away at my wine, when I feel someone sliding up beside me. He doesn't say anything until I turn to face him, to see who it is.

"Awrite, Lisa?" he says shyly. I recognise him but not enough to remember his name. He must have sensed my confusion, following up with, "It's Fraser, ah was the year above you at Coltness."

"Oh right, Fraser, ah remember you now. God you've changed, ah didn't recognise you there," I say, still trying to properly picture him.

"Aye, watching what ah eat these days," he says patting his stomach.

It was then I fully remember who he is. He's lost weight since school, and it definitely suits him. We start chatting away about school and what we're doing. He works in an electronics factory in the Netherton Industrial Estate. I tell him about my college and that. While we're talking, a crowd of girls has gathered round our table. Stubbsy and Eddie are lapping it up, but Stevie, as usual, is not showing any interest. I catch Stubbsy watching me talking with Fraser. What the fuck's his problem?

"Listen, ehm, Lisa, ah was wondering, if you maybe want to go out for a drink some time?"

"What, like a date?" I tease.

"Eh aye, aye a date," he says, blushing furiously.

I look over towards Stubbsy. His face is like thunder.

"Aye, here's my number," I say as I flick my phone open theatrically.

After exchanging numbers with Fraser I go back to the table. Stevie and Eddie start taking the piss a wee bit calling me a "wee minx"; they obviously saw me take Fraser's number. Then it happens. Stubbsy slams his bottle on the table, which causes the rest of the drinks to pile onto the floor. We all look at each other startled. A bouncer comes over to see what the commotion is. Stubbsy just stands up and brushes him aside.

"Too much ay that," Eddie says to the guy, sheepishly.

By this time, all eyes are on Stubbs as he moves towards the exit. Just as I think he's going to head out the door, the big bouncer that battered that lassie over in Hamilton comes towards him and tries to chummily pat him on the back. Stubbsy grabs his hand, swivels on his toes and cracks the big guy with the fastest punch I've ever seen. The other bouncers run towards the fracas, but Stubbsy stares them all down. One by one they all back off. The big bouncer is struggling to his feet, still not sure exactly what has happened. It's weird seeing him stand head and shoulders above Stubbsy, what with him always being taller than the rest of us.

Stubbsy hits him again. This time he falls to the ground and Stubbsy starts smashing the back of his heel into the top of his head till blood starts spurting all over the floor. When he finally finishes, he rubs his hands, looks right into my eyes, turns and walks out the door, leaving an exhilarated feeling in my stomach that I am not proud of. I run to the toilet, to try and gather my thoughts on my own. As I sit in the solace of the ladies, I try to work out what has just happened. Why was he looking at me when carrying out such violence? Why pick on someone so random? And why was I so turned on by such a heinous act? I sit in silence for a minute, until something brings me round sharply. It's muffled and, to be honest I can't be sure, but through the noise and the confusion outside, I swear I can hear people cheering.

CHAPTER 5

MARIE'S THE NAME

DO I REGRET WHAT I DID? YES. IN THAT SOBER WAKING-up-in-the-morning-could-I-take-it-all-back-way, yes, I wish to God I hadn't done it. I'd say it was out of character – even though it took character to do it, if you know what I mean. Picking up some guy in a bar and taking him back to our home? A complete stranger? That's bad in certain contexts; in others, it's despicable. But you know what? Despite the guilt, the worry and the awful knots in my stomach that linger and don't seem to be going away, I don't regret it. I wish I hadn't done it, obviously, but it's got Alistair and I doing something we haven't done in a long time. Me and Alistair are talking again. I'd love to say "talking after seven hours of mad, passionate love-making", but for now, I'll take talking. Of course, if you asked him, communication between both of us has been fine and dandy. It would be, if you regard decent conversation to involve the price war between Good and Evil, or Morrisons and Tesco as they are known in our house. I mean, he actually uses the term 'price war'.

"The price war between us and them got a wee bit more interesting today, hen. Whilst they've been caught short with their tired old 'buy-any-two-get-one-free' on selected frozen meals, we've went for the jugular. 'Buy-one-get-one-free-on-ALL-frozen-meals-till-the-end-of-the-month'!"

And I am sitting there looking at him and thinking, "Seriously, Alistair, screw me. Pretend I am one of those guns you use to price discounted items, take me up the stairs and have me any way you want!" But it rarely happens, and, if it does, it's about as predictable as the safety videos he shows to the new starts in his shop.

And this was the conversation I was having with Morag that fateful night in the Tavern when I stupidly did what I did. It was about quarter to two, just after lunch, when wee Dylan O'Conner came wandering into my class without knocking, idled up to my desk and handed me a piece of paper, walking back out without saying a word. Any other pupil in the school would have got a flea in the ear for not showing the expected decorum when entering another teacher's class, but wee Dylan was one of those dreamy, docile kids that gets away with such things and will probably do so for the rest of his life. The wee guy cracks me up and that's why Morag will always send him round with personal notes instead of simply sending me a text.

The note said, THEIR DAD'S GOT THE KIDS TONIGHT! U FANCY THE TAV, HON?

This has been a regular thing ever since Raymond and her split up. They're not divorced and it's supposed to be a big secret because it's a Catholic school, but I'm sure some of the teachers and even more of the parents are well up to speed. It didn't take me long to make my mind up. Alastair was working one of those daft split-shift things that meant he wouldn't be home till the early hours of the morning. Coming home at all hours on a Friday night? Morag kicked Raymond out for doing the same thing.

We headed down straight after work. We managed to catch the lunchtime menu which finished at half-four. The place was mobbed. The end-of-the-month brigade were there to make a dent in the green figure that shows on the ATM once the mortgage, council tax, credit cards and the rest have been savagely taken from their account. They all had a peculiar air of weekend expectancy and Morag and I were delighted to be a part of them. We started off on beers as it somehow felt too early to be drinking wine. But such reticence gradually eroded and the vino was, by six-thirty, softly catching the back of our throats and slowly numbing our arms and legs.

"So, m'lady, how'z you and the Alastair one getting on?" Morag teasingly asked, as she pointed her glass in my direction.

I was dreading her asking me that. I was so used to listening to the whole Morag and Raymond soap opera that I never had to explain what was, or was not, going on between Alastair and me. And that was the way I liked it. But the wine had dulled my senses and loosened my tongue. The more I drank, the more relaxed my inner defences became and before long I was pouring my heart out to her about everything. You see, in the past I never wanted to say anything to anybody because I always felt that by doing so I was somehow collaborating with the notion that Alastair and me were mismatched, an idea that I totally resented. But the more time went on, the more I began to believe it.

"Morag, things aren't good, to be honest." She widened her eyes and pulled her glass towards her chest, in what was a pretty good show of astonishment, but she was kidding nobody. She's silently known that I've been unhappy for a while now and never mentioned it, instead waiting for me to do the honours.

"Och, you know what he's like, Morag, with his job and everything. But it's getting me down."

Morag listened to me intently, occasionally trying to butt with some anecdote from her own marriage problems, but I was on a roll and wasn't stopping for anybody.

"I mean, it's not his job as such. If he was a big city computer analyst with major responsibilities I could accept him taking his work home and talking to me about it now and again. In fact, I would be glad to do that because that's what marriage is about, understanding each other the way no one else can. But honestly, Morag, the way he goes on about that fucking supermarket."

Morag nodded sympathetically and gently began her cross examination. "Is it just his job that bugs you Marie, or is it other things, because let's face it Alistair has always been a jobsworth. Ever since the day you met him. I mean, you did work with him up there, when it was Safeway. You must have known what he was like. But there's something else Marie, isn't there?" She gave me that teasing smile again, hoping to extract some illicit confession.

"Well yeah, there is actually. We don't have sex."

"Really, since when?"

"No Morag, we *don't* have sex."

"What, never?"

"In five years of marriage, I still don't have to use my toes to count. It's still in finger figures."

I could see that this had startled her. I'm sure she didn't think Alistair and I were at it morning, noon and night, but she obviously thought we were more active than that.

"Why have you put up with that for so long, Marie? I mean, ok, I think people do put too much emphasis on that side of a marriage, but it's got to be in there on some level. Don't get me wrong, Raymond and I were hardly swinging from the chandeliers, but we at least tried to enjoy each other whenever we could. So what are you going to do about it? Have you thought about counselling?"

"I want to have an affair, Morag."

I don't know why I said it. I didn't really want to have an affair, but I felt so frustrated. And the frustration was borne out of the sheer hopelessness of the situation. Alastair and I were talking, but not about the root of the problem. He thinks he just has to have sex with me more and then that will be that. But it's not only that. There's no closeness anymore. He doesn't hold me at night. He'll kiss me on the lips before he goes to work, but he'll never kiss me on the head when we're watching telly, or on the neck when I am getting ready in front of the mirror. I had to face up to the facts. Alastair didn't fancy me. And the most annoying thing about it was that he would never admit it.

So I had all these things going through my head and more wine in my system, when I saw him get up and come over towards our table. I thought at first he looked like Robert Redford, except much bigger, but when he got closer, I realized that he was nowhere near as handsome and his hair was much lighter. He swaggered up towards our table and sat down on the spare seat without looking in our direction. He leant his hand under the table and looked around shiftily, as if he was making sure no one could hear him.

"Don't worry girls, if you're overcome with passion and ye feel ye can't resist me, it's OK, and ah've got a rubber!" At which point he held up a Thomas the

Tank Engine pencil rubber that he'd swiped from the top of Morag's bag.

"Hey, that's theft!" Morag squealed, whilst nervously flicking her hair.

"Aye? You think that's theft. Two pound fuckin fifty for that pint a pish, that's theft!" he said, holding aloft an admittedly horrible looking pint of lager. He took a look at our bags that were stuffed with coloured card, glue, and a ton of jotters.

"So you guys are teachers then, aye? Ah said to ma pal Stevie over there, ah said, 'They're teachers mate, bet ye they are'. So what are your names then?"

At this Morag sat up, pushed her chest out slightly and beamed the introductions. "I'm Morag and this is my friend, Marie."

He politely shook both our hands, discretely clocking the ring on my wedding finger and discreetly turned his attentions to Morag.

"Morag? Nice name, like it. Morag what?"

Morag lowered her eyes and shrunk into herself.

"It's Morag Ringtool, actually, but don't bother, I've heard all the jokes!" she said quietly.

"Don't know any Morag jokes am afraid. So what we up to tonight then?"

And that was it. One wee funny comment and he had us. His name was Gary Stubbs, or Stubbsy. He was nice. Very confident and flirtatious, but not in a boring, predictable way. He wasn't full on like some guys are, the ones who feel they have to come up with a funny innuendo to everything that's been said. He made us laugh, but he could relax enough to have a normal conversation. He worked over in Hamilton as an electrician, which Morag thought was "handy". She fancied him, there was no doubt about that, and I was happy for her. She hadn't been with anyone since Raymond and she deserved a bit of fun. He left briefly to go and say goodbye to his mates, one of which was a blonde girl. The other was some guy with dark hair, who I assumed was the Stevie he was going on about, but I didn't get a proper look at him. When he got back to our table he picked up his drink and downed it in one.

"Right, whit's happenin', shite in here. Fancy movin' on?"

Morag looked at me hesitantly, as if she wanted my permission to ask him back to her place. I didn't mind at all but I was leaving them to it. I'd had a good night, but I didn't want to be a gooseberry.

"Ehm, I've got some drink at the house, we could go back there if you want?" Morag said to both of us.

"Na, you two go, I'd best be getting back for my hubby coming home. You can drop me off in the taxi though." As I said this, Morag looked at me apologetically, as if to say "Are you sure?" but I think she was secretly pleased.

We didn't have to wait long for a cab as it was only about ten o'clock. In the taxi, Morag and Stubbsy sat next to each other, Stubbsy cracking some lame jokes with the driver as Morag giggled like a schoolgirl. I sat there enjoying the hazy drunk feeling only a certain class of white wine can give you. As we got to the roundabout at Flemington, Morag's phone began to vibrate. She clumsily prised the phone from her bag and squinted at the name that was illuminating before her. Her face dropped as she read who it was.

"Raymond? What's wrong?"

At this Stubbsy and I looked at each other nervously, awaiting some bad news. Morag looked deflated as she slipped her mobile down.

"Sorry guys going to have to take a rain check. Jennifer's got a temperature and he can't get her to sleep. I'll have to go see she's ok. Sorry."

I told her it was ok and asked the driver to take a detour to the flats at the old Wishaw High School. Stubbsy just sat there trying not to look to uncomfortable.

When we got to Raymond's place Morag apologized to Stubbsy and half-heartedly reminded him that he had her number and that he could call her any time, at which Stubbsy gave her a reassuring thumbs up.

"So what now?" Stubbsy said to me, as innocently as he could.

"What now, mister, is you drop me off at my house and get the nice wee taxi man here to take you home," I said, trying my hardest not sound like a school teacher.

"Ok miss, it's just it's a bit early, and you said your man won't be back till after twelve. Any drink in the house?"

I stared at him for a couple of seconds to see if he was really serious.

"Oh c'mon, Marie, relax man. Ahm not tryin to fire into you, well, ah thought about it earlier, but c'mon it's no even half ten yet. Wee glass ay wine at yours, how about it?"

As he said this I started to smile despite myself, the way I do every time wee Dylan from Morag's class comes into mine.

"One glass, cowboy, then its home time," I said, stupidly relenting to his charm.

"Once the bell goes, miss, no problem," he replied, whilst sensibly ignoring the winking taxi driver.

When we got back to my place, we hurriedly ran to the front door, which was unnecessary as most of the people round here had young kids and had climbed the stairs with exhaustion hours ago, getting ready for a new day of mayhem. I ushered Stubbsy into the kitchen through the front entrance of the house. I took his jacket and showed him to the living room, all the time wondering what the hell I was doing.

"Nice gaff, looks nothing like ah thought it would be," he grinned while absorbing my obvious cream-carpet, brown-leather-suite, sparkle-lamps style living room. He knew how to take the piss, I'd give him that. I poured the wine and handed him his glass. I couldn't help thinking what Alastair would do. And that was the problem; I didn't know what he would do. As much as I tried to picture Alastair, who didn't have a violent bone in his body, physically manhandling Stubbsy off the premises, the image was simply too ridiculous.

"So who's the blonde girl?" I said to him for no other reason than trying to keep the conversation light.

"Who Lisa? Fuckin nut job. Stays with ma mate Stevie, found out last year her sister was actually her mam and her mam was actually her gran, if you know what I mean."

"That must have been awful," I said with as much concern as possible, even though I didn't know her.

"Aye it was, but, c'mon, we've all got problems, and least her mam's still on the go. Stevie's mam fucked off and left when he was about ten, leaving him wi just his da. And anyway it disnae excuse her behaviour. Ah mean last week, we're in the town going round a few bars in that. She spots some guy she recognized from the college. Cut a long story short, by the end of the night, she's slow-dancin' wi this clown, lettin him nuzzle away at her neck!"

"What's wrong with that?" I protested.

"She was supposed to be with us!" he said indignantly.

"Stubbsy, have you ever considered the idea that the reason you get so angry with this girl is because you actually fancy her?"

"What the fuck was that?"

Stubbsy was now on his feet, peering out the window at the car that I already had recognized to be Alastair's.

"It's Alastair," I said calmly as I took a large gulp of wine.

"Your husband? Fuck! Right, backdoor, ahm out of here!" But I stood in his way, took his hand and pointed towards the front door.

"Stubbsy, go out the door you came in, please."

"But what's he going to say when he sees me leave for fuck sake?" he hissed quietly.

"I don't know, but I want to find out."

He looked at me like I had lost my mind or that I was somehow playing some sick joke. It wasn't till he saw the determination on my face that he realized I was serious, and that by letting Alastair know he was in the house he was actually doing me a big favour. He stood for a minute and stared, slightly confused. Then he smiled at me, winked and shook his head. I didn't have to say, but, in his own way, he seemed to understand. Stubbsy put on his jacket and walked out the house without a shred of fear.

Alastair came running breathlessly past him into the house.

"You ok hen?" he asked, but as he looked around and noticed the lights still on in the living room, two wine glasses half drunk, and 'The Sundays' album purring on the background, he realized things where far from ok.

"Alastair, honey," I said "We need to talk…"

CHAPTER 6

TEARS THAT TOOK HIM NOWHERE

MY DAD WASN'T A BIG DRINKER. He enjoyed the odd drink and I enjoyed *him* enjoying the odd drink. Whilst most kids were embarrassed when their parents indulged in a tipple (or in some more unfortunate cases, frightened), I used to look forward to it. I can always remember when he used to reach into the drinks cabinet at the back of the living room and pull out a bottle of red wine (it was always wine, he never drank beer or spirits) and me thinking, "Good. He'll maybe talk to me now; maybe even play with me for a wee bit."

One time in particular he had finished a bottle of claret and was well into his second. He picked me up on his knee and began ruffling my hair and tickling me till I couldn't breathe with hysterics. This was before my mam had left us and he was generally less uptight. Once the hilarity had died down, he reverted back to Mister Serious.

"Steven, son, you know I love you dearly and I will always provide for you and your mum. When you're studying, and you will study when you're older, you won't need to work, never. I will not allow it, do you understand that Steven?"

I just nodded and soaked up this rare show of affection for what it was worth. Financial stability may not win you Father of the Year, but for him it was the most he could offer and I suppose, at the time, he genuinely meant it.

Morrisons Wishaw was my first real job as such. It was part-time and it provided much needed back-up finance to the allowance Dad sent home from Australia. Wednesday was my day off at the college, so I made myself available for any shifts going.

I work in the Replenishment bit which is everything that's not produce, bakery or booze. It's a crap job, but it's easy. The work itself isn't taxing, but the people I work with most certainly are. Anyone who takes up a career in the supermarket trade through choice should be tagged and monitored because those people have dangerous mindsets that must never be ignored.

On my usual shift, it's predominantly young part-timers who think Jackass are the new Beatles. They spend the most part of their shift crowded around a mobile phone while some hero shows them a perma-tanned American porn star getting rogered stupid in an L.A. studio, whilst trying to persuade the rest of the boys that it's all happening down the road somewhere.

"See that there? That's the lassies' toilets in Motherwell Point. The middle bit. Oh aye, our Jojo's mate shagged her roon the back ay the Aquatec one night," and the goons either believe it or pretend to believe because they live in Wishaw, a place where individual thought is frowned upon and stamped out at birth. I don't know what they think of me, I've hardly spoken to any of them, but needless to say I am known as "that guy whose mad bird topped herself".

The day shift is different, however. It's mainly full-timers. Most of them are older and have worked here for years. There are others who, worryingly, started off part-time to get them through their degrees and ended up here full-time when they realized there was up a dry-up in the market for Scottish Literature Engineers. These are the ones who end up in a position of superiority, whilst the older generation are happy to let them get on with it.

The most annoying of these old timers is a guy called Andy, or "ANDREW!" as the old dears call him after he's made some half-arsed attempt at innuendo, which is the reason why I find him so annoying. He works in the Environmental Maintenance Department, which means if someone drops a jar of chopped tomatoes he has to go clean it up. As I'm not usually on at this time, he believes he has an untapped audience for his crass sense of humour. It's when I'm filling up my replenishment trolley with the two litre Diet Irn Bru that the unholy diatribe begins.

"AGNES!" he shouts towards the bakery section, hands on hips and a sideway smile beginning to form on his old, decrepit mouth. "THERE'S SOMETHING OLD AND DIRTY UP HERE NEEDIN SEEIN TAE!" He shows me his filthy mop and winks, as if he's being dead cunning.

"Oh Andrew, you've got something up yer sleeve, you always have," Agnes says coyly.

"ONLY THE ARMS THAT LONG TO HOLD YOU, AGNES, THE ARMS THAT LONG TO HOLD YOU!" Which is met by wild cackles from the bakery department, as Andrew waddles his way onto the shop floor with a grin the size of the queue at the basket counter. I smile weakly and put my head down and try and get on with my work without anyone noticing me.

The day goes by quickly enough. The day shift is better, in that there is always something to do. The worst thing about doing a job like this is standing about trying to look busy. I'm about to clean up my empty boxes and take them to the compactor, when a young girl nervously approaches me.

At first, I don't know if it's me she wants to talk to, as she's just standing behind me and waiting till I turn round. I see on her name badge that she's called

Tracy and the first thing that I notice about her is how un-Tracy-like she is. In fact, if it wasn't for the all-in-one dress she's wearing, I'd have sworn she's a pre-pubescent boy.

"Em, are you Steve?"

"Stevie, aye, what can ah do for you?" I say as relaxed as I can be in the hope that this kid will calm down a bit. Her face is scarlet.

"Ehm, Mr... eh... Alistair wants to see you in his office when you get a minute," she says as she points up the stairs.

"Eh aye ok, ah'll, eh head up once am done here. Thanks."

She moves away without any more acknowledgement, leaving me wondering what the hell the Assistant Manager wants me for. I've only been here two weeks and thought I was doing ok. Alistair is the dude that interviewed me for this job. The first impression I got of him was that he was a total jobsworth, but in an honest, earnest way. He seemed to be very excited about what was happening in the store. He had a vulnerability about him that made me think that all his best intentions would go unnoticed and he would be hated for being so dedicated to his job. After a week, my fears were confirmed. The workers, to a fucking man, hate the guy. They hate the fact he expects the same dedication for the job as he has, a job they find tedious and unrewarding. When you consider the nature of the work they are being asked to do, in relation to the money they are getting paid, you can't blame them really.

I take the steps two at a time and stride confidently towards Alistair's office. The confidence coming from the fact that there's been nothing I've done in the last two weeks this guy could be unhappy about.

"Steve!" he yells as I walk into the room. Don't know where this "Steve" comes from. He's talking to me while fiddling about with his computer.

"With you in a minute. Right, all done. So?" He swings his chair towards me and clasps his hands together.

"How are you settling in Steve?"

"Eh aye awrite ah suppose, no problems so far," I shrug.

"You're doing well down there, Steve, I've been hearing nothing but good reports, mate." His use of the word "mate" is a little too chummy for my liking. "Yep, it's rare for a part-time employee to pick up the logistics of the job so easily and in such a short space of time. We usually give them a few months to bed in, but Bruce, your team leader, tells me he's been leaving you unsupervised with important tasks he wouldn't leave in the hands of a seasoned full-timer."

Seasoned full-timer? For fuck's sake.

"Just doing what ah'm told, Alistair, nothing more than that," I say as he sits back on his chair, presidentially waving his finger in my direction.

"Ah, but it's more than that though, Steve, believe me. You see, it's not just my job to look after this store on a day to day basis; there are other things I have to consider. If you can show me a more cut-throat business than the one we find ourselves in at the moment, then I'll eat my Stetson."

This cunt's patter? No wonder everybody hates him.

"We have to keep moving, keep things fresh. Stand still and our competitors will kill us. I have to spot potential, Steve, people who could, in the future, take this place forward. I am not going to be here forever."

This is unbelievable; the guy's twenty-six, twenty-seven tops, and he's already trying to groom me as his successor. The cunt's mad.

"Look, Alistair," I say, trying to find a balance between non-committal and flattery, "ah don't mind this job, ah try my best because ah find that by doing that, people like you tend to keep off my back. But, honestly, ah couldn't ever see a time when I could throw myself into this job, or any job, the way you do. Ah enjoy my studies; ah want to hopefully find a decent career path through them. Until then ah'll obviously do my bit up here, but ahm a part-time worker, and that's how it's going to stay."

He looks at me for a second, his hands in front of his nose in prayer mode.

"Well, it's something to think about, ay? I mean we never know what's going to happen next do we?" At this point he squints at the security images on the is behind him. "Ah, Marie, my wife, she's early. She used to work in here as well, but like you, she had ambitions elsewhere." I take this as a cue to leave.

"Eh, see you later, Alistair," I half mumble.

"Oh yes Steve, catch you later mate," he says as he zips back into life after staring at the screen showing the aisle that his wife was walking up.

That was murder. I feel bad for Alistair. A good guy caught in the wrong time zone or country or something, I don't know. I am walking down the stairs from Alistair's office, mentally preparing myself for another heavy topic of conversation. Something tells me that the discussion I've just had with him will be a breeze compared to the one I am due to have later. My lecturer, Carolyn, has set up a session with the counselling lecturer at the College. She feels it would be beneficial for me to talk about how I am and how I feel after Clare's death. I was reluctant to do it, but Carolyn's been good to me so for her sake I said I'd give it a go.

"Honestly, man, e-mail your answers to the usual address, www.whitthefuckshedainmarriedtaethatprick.com."

Glenn and Stuart, two wee part-timers, are about to start their shift, but take time out to stare down the bakery aisle at what must be Alistair's wife.

"Enjoy yer shift, boys!" I say as I make my way to the Bakery, hoping to catch a swatch at Alistair's wife. I've heard she's a stunner, which I don't believe. This is Alistair we're talking about, and this is Wishaw, where expectations of attractiveness are significantly lower than anywhere else in the Western world. By the time I get there, the aisle is empty. I consider doing a tour of the shop to see if can see her, but realise what a Royal Wank ay' Scotland that would make me. I buy myself a wee water from the kiosk and make my way down to the college for some old fashioned therapy.

The college is empty; it's that time of the day when the full-time students have all gone, while those doing night classes haven't arrived. I make my way through the sterile corridors past pictures of long-dead MPs shaking hands with long-retired Rectors and opening up long-condemned wings of the college. I lose my way, as I've no idea where I am actually going. When I eventually arrive at the office of the woman I am supposed to meet, I'm met with a familiar vision. The lecturer that old Sam and Davie keep bangin on about is sitting at her desk. She's wearing glasses and, despite it being early evening, she still looks like she's walked straight out of a beauty salon.

"Hi there, eh ahm Steve, eh Stevie. Carolyn asked, eh said ah should..."

"Come in, come in. You're early, haven't quite prepared for you yet. Coffee?"

"Aye, go on then, milk one sugar. Just want me to sit here, aye?"

"Yeah, here's fine, nothing formal today, just a chat about how you're doing."

I don't like the way she said "today", it almost implies that this isn't a one-off. She definitely seems nice enough, which is part of her job I suppose, but I don't feel comfortable. I had resolved to be as open as I can with her, but I didn't think sitting here talking about what happened can make me feel any better about it. In my own mind I've had conversations with myself about every possibility, eventuality and outcome and it hasn't made the slightest bit of difference.

"Ok Stevie, I'm Linda, trained counsellor, and what you're here for today is to try and go through various things that have happened, how you feel about what's happened, and how we can make you feel better about it. Now, if this was a formal counselling session we would have to agree on certain boundaries, which is a common practice that safeguards both counsellor and client, but as this is an informal chat we can get straight to the specifics. Now, are you comfortable with that?"

"Ehm, aye, aye ah am."

I was going to say, "Actually no, ah think this is a waste of both our times," but decide to let it flow and hope it doesn't last too long.

"Ok Stevie, Carolyn asked me to have this chat with you because she feels that you haven't coped properly with the recent tragic events that have occurred in your life. Your girlfriend committed suicide. No one really knows why. Usually this would send an individual into a period of mourning, of anger or resentment. But according to Carolyn you have not showed any of these feelings. Now, I don't know why this is the case, and I am willing to bet that you don't know either. So tell me, Stevie, how are you feeling, generally?"

I feel a cold sweat run down my back. I thought we were going to talk about the hows, the whys and the wheres. I should tell her about the dreams, but that would open up a street I don't want to go down. But at the same time, she's a professional, she might know why I am having these dreams. But then she'll want to know about Mam and that and I can't face that. Fuck it. I'll tell the truth, say how I feel and if it helps then fine, if not, then no one can say I didn't try.

"Well, am not coping to be honest with you, Linda, but it's just that crying and moaning about it would only make me feel worse. Ah prefer to keep a lid on things, y'know?" She looks at me and smiles as if she knew this was what I was going to say. Three rules of counselling: never give advice, never ask a question you don't know the answer to, and never ever charge under twenty-five quid an hour. Linda would only break one of these rules tonight.

"Keeping it locked inside, that's a typical trait amongst most men. In working-class areas, this trait is more prevalent. In working-class Scotland, it's almost compulsory. Some people believe it to be a bad thing, but let's face it, if the world was full of wailing men bearing their souls every five minutes we would all be in a lot of trouble. There's nothing wrong with letting other people think you're ok, the problem arises when you start to convince yourself that you're ok when clearly you're not. I hope you don't mind, but I spoke with your flatmate, Lisa. She tells me that at the service for Clare you didn't cry; in fact, you showed no emotion at all."

"Aye, ah bet she did," I say raising my eyebrows.

"She's worried about you, Stevie, and her worries seem to stem from the same ones Carolyn has; your lack of emotion towards what is a highly emotive occurrence." She's getting somewhere, no doubt about it. I don't like being portrayed as heartless, or as someone that doesn't care. I have my reasons, good reasons, and it's all to do wi ma mam.

"My mam left me when ah was ten."

Again the smile; I've fallen into her trap.

"Tell me about that."

I don't want to, I never have before and the reason for that is that I can't properly rationalize it out in my own mind.

"Came home from school one night and my Aunty May, my dad's sister, was in the house with my dad. They were looking at a note on the breakfast bar that was obviously from my mam. Aunt May looked like she had been crying, whilst Dad kept running his hands through his hair, looking totally shattered. He left it to Aunt May to tell me. She said that Mam was away for a bit, but she would be home soon. Ah couldn't work it out. Why would she go away without saying goodbye? Ah cried for days. And what made it worse, was that Dad would just ghost about the house like a zombie. Every time ah tried to talk to him it would be like, 'Not now Steven,' and so ah would just go up to ma bed and cry. Cry ma fuckin eyes out, and say daft wee prayers, 'Dear God, can you tell my mam to come home, she's been away for a week and two days and me and my dad want to her to come home.' But she never did. So there you go, crying gets you fuckin nowhere."

I find myself shaking, thinking about how Mam just went out and left us. I keep that to myself, but in here, talking to this professional, I'm letting my anger get the better of me.

"What is your feeling towards your mum now?" Linda asks quietly.

"Ah don't know really, there's times when ah think she must have been a pretty lousy, selfish person to walk out on us like that. But there are other times when ah think she was quite bold for doing what she did."

"In a good way?" Linda asks intently.

"Aye, definitely. Ah mean, she obviously wasn't happy with her lot, clearly didn't love my dad, and made the decision that she was going to make herself happy, despite the pain that would cause those around her. Now as self-centred as that may sound, when you think about it, you only get one shot at this gig. What's the point in allowing the only life you have be consumed by discontent. The way ah see it, by all means, love thy neighbour, but don't love him more than you love yourself." I can see she is a bit taken aback by this, and to be honest so am I, but I meant every word.

"And how does this relate to your feelings towards Clare and how she exited from your life? You must have realised the similarities?" Linda professionally inquires, making me feel like Anthony Soprano from the New Jersey family.

I twitch nervously. This was something I definitely had thought about. Thought about it a lot actually. "Ah think it's the same, man, honestly."

"In what way?" she asks.

"In that she stood up to the sadness. Whatever it was that was making her unhappy she stood up to it." I feel my hands shake as the room suddenly seems to go cold. I don't actually know why Clare took her life. What nobody knows is that, a couple of weeks before she went missing, she and I split up. It was mutual decision, though, and she seemed to think it was for the best. It was a decision that, at the time, I wouldn't have thought would have made her feel suicidal, which is why I still don't have the answer as to why she did it.

"So you think she was brave in taking her own life?"

"Ah think anyone who takes their own life is a fuckin hero. They are basically putting the middle finger up and saying, 'Fuck you, ah will not be unhappy anymore'."

I can feel the anger start to rise within me and, though I know I should quit while I'm ahead, I feel like I've been given a microphone to the world and want to shout my insides out. "Ah mean take a look around you, man," I say as I point out the window towards Motherwell town centre, "this town, it's a fuckin dump. Everywhere you look negativity stares back at you. Bookies and bingo halls thrive, while cafés and record shops fall by the wayside. Do you know Nick Cave? As in Nick Cave and the Badseeds?"

"Of course I do, yes," Linda answers, puzzled.

"He played in the Civic a few years back. Now, am not a massive fan ay the guy, but ah went cause he's a legend. This was the biggest star to ever play here. Do you know, on the night of the gig, you could have walked off the street and paid at the door. And the whole night ah didn't see one familiar face. An icon comes to your hometown and the natives are down the Miners giving it 'Brown Eyed Girl'."

Linda smiles almost to herself and looks me square in the eye. "Ok, hold on, but that doesn't explain your reticence when it comes to showing your emotions. Do you think you're displacing your anger and frustration at what happened with your mum and girlfriend at society in general?"

"Ahm not angry, ahm just disappointed. Disappointed that ah've lost someone who, despite everything, was a good friend. Disappointed that a brilliant man like Jack Murray has lost a daughter, after selflessly giving the best part of his life to help other people. But, most of all, am disappointed in myself. Because ah know that if ah was ever faced with the same kind of heartache she must have been feeling, ah wouldn't have the bottle to do something about it."

I can tell that what I've said has Linda intrigued. I mean it though, I really do. We speak some more about my friendship with Stubbsy and Lisa, and if I thought that I had sought these friendships out as a kind of substitute for my mam who fucked off when I was a kid, and my dad who couldn't bring me up on his own and had left for Australia with his new partner a week after my sixteenth birthday. I tell her that, no, that isn't the case; that Stubbsy is my mate because he makes me laugh more than anyone ever could, and that my friendship with Lisa is based on an unswerving respect I have for the way she is completely vulnerable and unsure until the moment when she needs to stand up and be counted, and at that point she becomes the strongest person I have ever known.

Carolyn wraps up our little meeting by asking me to think about certain things in a certain way, and arranges for a more formal session in a fortnight's time. I go along with it, but have no intention of coming back to see her. I respect her and am glad we had a chat. It's good to talk and all that. But I wasn't going to embark on a full programme of counselling. It doesn't fit with my outlook on things. It would invade into my thoughts on other subjects, like politics, race and religion. And besides, what would Stubbsy say?

Motherwell is accompanied by a familiar drizzly rain as I walk down to the Tav for a pint before heading home. At Grange Road, near Fir Park Stadium, I nearly bump into an old tramp who's slurping greedily at a half bottle of cheap cider.

"Cheer up son, fir fuck sake!" he shouts, trying to grab my arm. "It's a shithole, right enough, son, ay the old Motherwell," he says as he outstretches his arms like a preaching holy man.

"Aye, some place," I reply half-heartedly.

"Know the best thing ever tae come oot ay this shithole of a town, ay?" he asks, winking at me. I can feel a punch line coming that will leave one of the participants in this conversation in unbridled hysterics.

"The eight-fifty ay King's Cross, ay, ha, gittit? gittit?" I offer up a weak, fake laugh and leave him to his merriment. The problem was I did get it; I got it more than anyone could ever know.

CHAPTER 7

WISHAW DAME IF IT'S ALL THE SAME

It's six o'clock and it's still light outside! How good is that? I'm sitting at the dinner table, trying to do some of ma History essay, but I'm too distracted. I'm off out on a date tonight. Going for a drink with that Fraser guy I met at the Beer Festival. He seemed really nice, a bit forward, but he made me laugh. We'll see how it goes. Stubbsy says he's a prick and that I should be careful, but he's just saying that because Fraser's a Rangers supporter, and besides, the day I start taking lifestyle advice from that obnoxious prick is the day I die, sister!

I'm feeling all nice and deliberating on whether to have a cheeky wee wine or not, when Stevie comes down the stairs and into the living room. He's got nothing on except a pair of football shorts. I find myself staring at his torso, perfectly toned, even though he's never stepped foot in a gym in his life, and skin slightly tanned, even though he's hasn't been abroad in six years. I start to think of what his mam would have looked like. She must have been a beautiful woman to have produced a boy who was so naturally good looking.

As I stare at him, I start to laugh, despite myself. He looks round, and gives me a funny look, as if to say, "What the fuck you laughing at, you mad bitch?" But I just wave my hand to tell him it's nothing. I was laughing at how I wasn't attracted to him. Like most girls, he's the type of guy I would go for in a minute, but for some reason, there's nothing.

I can remember one night I was sitting in the flat on my own. I'd just got home from the gym and was feeling unusually horny for a nice girl like me! Stevie came in from the pub – pissed drunk – and lay down on the couch and fell asleep. As he lay there, I could see the top of his midriff, which was exposed above his belt. I sat there for ages looking at it thinking, "Ah could undo that belt and go down, down, down. Too right ah could!" But I didn't and I'm so glad of that. Sex complicates things, and Stevie's my best pal in the world. He seems to be getting over the whole Clare thing, which is good because I so don't want to talk about that.

I'm ready for the off surprisingly quickly. As usual, though, I never know what to wear on dates. On dates! Listen to me, Bridget Jones here, beating the boys off with a stick, ha ha! After much deliberation,

I opt for my tight black jeans I got from Gap, with my long grey top with a white belt I got from Accessorize. Casual, but smart; can't go wrong with that. We've arranged to meet in Starka, which made Stevie laugh. He says everyone in Motherwell goes to Starka on their first date. He says you can tell them apart from the other couples in the way they look at each other, all full of interest and good intention, whereas the ones who have been together for a time are usually sitting with blank bored expressions. I love Stevie to bits, but sometimes I think he's too cynical. He's really clever, but sometimes a bit too clever, do you know what I mean?

Ahm havin' a wine! I know, I know, but I've got that mad nervous feelin' you get pre-first-date. Mad thoughts. We don't really know each other, what are we gonnae talk about for four hours. What does he look like? Mental, ah cannae even remember! I've often wondered if guys think like this as well. It never seems like it. It's like they've just turned up without giving it as much as a thought. Or maybe that's a front. If us girls are honest, it's them that have to put in the leg work, they have to impress us. The poor souls.

The other reason am feeling anxious is my dad. Ma real dad. I made contact yesterday. It wasn't as hard as I thought it was. His name is Douglas, or Dougie. Apparently his mum has been trying to make contact with me for some time and has been leaving phone numbers and forwarding addresses in the hope I would get in touch. Ma mam, or rather ma gran, has been keeping this from me, which didn't surprise or anger me. I'd made my peace with her and reasoned that anything she had done in the past, rightly or wrongly, she did with my best intentions in mind. And besides, I wanted to do this without any fallouts or hang ups. So I did it. I dialled the number and waited to hear my dad's voice for the first time. I had hoped that someone else would answer first, so that I could tell them who I was, so that he would be pre-warned. But no, it was him. His voice. My dad. It was weird. He didn't seem shocked or surprised. But to be honest, he didn't sound too pleased either. He was kind of nonplussed, but we arranged to meet. Next week. So we'll see.

I phone a taxi five minutes after am supposed to meet Fraser, which means I will be exactly fifteen fashionable minutes late. Stevie comes through and wishes me luck, tells me to be careful, to phone him at any time if I need to. If my real dad cares for me as much as Stevie does, I'll be onto a right winner.

I walk through the double glass doors into a nearly deserted Starka. Fraser is how I remembered him. Tallish with black gelled hair, small darting eyes and a wee beer belly popping through his Burton or Next striped shirt. He smiles when he sees me and gets up from his chair.

"Hiya, eh, what you wantin'?" he says nervously. I can see small sweat patches under his arms, which tell me he's as nervous as I am.

"A medium white wine, please," I reply as calmly as possible.

And that was it, we were away. The conversation ranged from all the different people we both knew to his work and my college. It was ok, nice even, but after about two hours I knew that this was the last time I would be seeing the bold Fraser. He was a decent type, I suppose, but I didn't have a good feeling about him. At one point, he spoke about the Orange flute band he played in for at least half an hour, despite me telling him I wasn't interested in any of that shit. But still he went on.

"It's a buzz though, aw they folk, who you know are all the same, they're there ay see you playin' tunes that represent yer religion, where ye come fae, plus ye git tae piss the local bead rattlers aff, which is always a good thing."

And so this goes on and on. I begin lookin' at my watch, which he seems oblivious to. Then he says something that, for some reason, makes me really angry. To try and steer him away from the bigoted garbage he was spewing, I ask him if he knows Stevie. They're around the same age and went to the same school.

"Oh aye, ah know him," he says in a somewhat sly manner.

"You sound a bit apprehensive, you know ah share a flat with him? He's a good friend."

"Eh naw, it's not that. He's awrite actually, Stevie, shame about that bird he was seein'. Naw it's his big mate ah don't like. That Fenian bastard, Stubbsy. Him and his family should go back to the country they came fae. Next time ye see him, tell him 'the famine's over, it's time to go home'." He's half-slurring, half-laughing at this till he sees my face, which is like thunder.

Now, there's no one hates big Stubbsy more than me. I always think he childishly resents my friendship with Stevie. He constantly puts me down in front of people and makes snide remarks about everything from my appearance to my opinion on, well, anything. But what I do know is that he is a proud individual who always looks out for his friends and would never let anyone talk them down.

"Ah'll tell him that," I say frostily as possible, letting him know that I'm not impressed.

"Naw man, ah was only joking. C'mon lets finish these and head over ay The Edge," he says as he squeezes my knee, which I respond to with a short glance at his hand, then a scowl in his direction.

I'm thinking I should head home now, but I decide to go over to the club and hopefully meet some randoms I can slinky in with and maybe he'll get the message. The club, unlike Starka, is bouncing. I feel him grab my waist as we manoeuvre ourselves through the crowd. His touch chills me and I pull myself from him as we reach the bar area. He goes to get the drinks and I have a quick but studious scan of the place in the vain hope of seeing someone I know. No luck.

The DJ is blasting out some moronic, cheesy Ibiza music that makes me think again of Stevie. It's hard to put it into words; in fact, mere words could never do justice to how much he hates places like this. He came in once for a college night out and I honestly thought he was going to burst into tears. Whilst scanning the balcony area my attention is brought to the edge of the dance floor where a hilarious vision has caught my eye. A fattish, balding bloke in his late thirties, dressed like he's just spent forty quid worth of BHS vouchers in the men's department, is stood behind this young girl, hands on each side of her face, grinding like some west coast hip-hop artist and the girl – who can't be more than nineteen years old – is looking left to right, absolutely petrified, hoping one of her pals will come and rescue her.

Fraser comes back from the bar and asks me to dance. Before I have a chance to say "No", he drags me up on the dance floor. I try my best to look interested as he moves awkwardly to the music. Every now and then, he tries to push up close to me, trying to grab my arse and kiss my neck. Each time I push him away he waits for a bit, then comes on again. Eventually he gets the hint and shoves me away and says something that sounds like "whore" and turns his attention to some fat girl who's plastered in glitter. Lucky girl.

With relief I head off the dance floor and go to get my coat from the cloakroom without looking round. As I'm waiting on the girl getting my jacket, I can feel sweat running down my back and my ears. I'm feeling tired and I want to go home. Just then he appears. Grabbing hold of my arm he spins me round to face him.

"Hey gorgeous, where you going?" He's leering at me now and for the first time I'm beginning to feel a little scared.

"Am going home, Fraser. It was a nice night thanks, but ah'll be heading off now." He looks me up and down for a bit, then eventually lets go of my arm, and puts his hands up in surrender mode.

"Ok, no worries, thank you too, it's been a good night. Ah'll walk you to the rank."

"No it's ok honestly, it's just round the corner," I'm pleading.

"Och don't be daft, come on before you turn into a pumpkin."

Once outside, the fresh air is welcomingly cooler and the taxi rank is only yards away. I'm trying to walk as briskly as I can, hoping he'll take the hint and turn away in the opposite direction. But as I'm about to turn onto the side street where the rank is, I feel a sharp tug at my wrist. Before I can react, Frazer has pulled me into a shop doorway and is standing in front of me with his hands clasped tightly to my arms. He takes a step back, looks me up and down and winks at me.

"How about a wee kiss then, gorgeous?" he says, glancing towards his groin area.

"Fuck off, you prick, and leave me alone," I say as I try to barge past him, but he pushes me back to the spot directly in front of him.

"C'mon tae fuck man, ah've seen ye out about, always wi guys, lovin the attention. Tryin' tae tell me your no suckin' yer pal Stevie tae sleep every night, eh? There's lassies out there, especially the ones that hing aroon' the band when we play, that would love to be in your position."

I don't know what I feel most: fear or anger. All I know is that I am in big trouble and have to get away from him immediately. He tries to grab me again, this time by the hips. He's let go of my arms, which gives me some vital leverage. I remember Stubbsy saying once that if you're on top of someone and you really want to hurt them, a thumb in the eye is always better than a fist to the jaw. Despite being sickened by the violence of such a statement, I was going to heed that advice tonight. By now, he's up against me trying to kiss me on the mouth. I manage to place my right hand on his face and crawl my finger nails, spider-like up towards his eyes. Before he has a chance to move away, I dig my pinkie nail right in his eye. At first it seems like I haven't hurt him, until I hear him scream out a searing yelp.

"AHH, FUCKIN, YA BITCH, FUCKIN EYE!" I dash out on to the street hoping to be met by a policeman, a courting couple, or even some girls on their way home. Instead I run into a team of young, drunk guys, about seventeen, eighteen. I fall breathlessly in amongst them, to a chorus of wolf whistles and derogatory remarks. Just as I am thinking, "Out of the frying pan," I feel a cold, sweaty hand on my shoulder. I turn round to see a skinny ginger-haired kid with bad acne looking deep into my eyes. I start to notice that his eyes aren't glazed like his friends', and his breath is free of any stale alcohol. More importantly, I notice the jingling car keys he has in his other hand. He's sober! Thank God for the designated driver!

"Are you ok?" he asks nervously.

"Taxi." I'm panting heavily.

"Aye, sure, c'mon I'll walk you up," he says, giving the peace sign to his wee mates, which I take to mean two minutes. His mates start egging him on, making him blush, but I couldn't care less; he was ma wee saviour tonight and I'm eternally grateful.

"Go on Dempsey boy, get in there!" they shout, as we join the end of the taxi queue.

"Em, ah've got my car, well Dad's car here, if you want a lift?" He speaks with a polite, posh manner that makes me think he comes from a wealthy respectable family. His actions and willingness to help me doesn't make me think any different.

"No, it's fine, you go get your friends, thank you."

"If you're sure?"

"Yeah, honestly, here's a cab coming now."

"Ok, bye then."

"Thanks again." Wee angel. He's saved me here, thank God. The taxi driver is unusually quiet, which is good. I am angry, tired and pissed off. That prick tried to rape me. Would he have stopped? It didn't feel like it.

Fuckin' men. I do pick them. What's the matter with me? The taxi swerves into the car park of our tenement flat and I pay the driver plus a wee tip. I'm in the lift and suddenly become anxious. I am struggling to breathe and feel as if the whole lift shaft is going to topple on top of me. When the doors slide open I fall out onto the landing and start to cry. I feel horrible. Those disgusting things he said about me. Did other people think that? Was I seen as some kind of slag because I went to the pub with the boys?

I struggle to get my key in the lock as my hands are still shaking. I can hear the TV coming from the living room. Stevie must still be up. Oh no. He'll want a run down on tonight and he'll know that something is wrong. I can't face him. I take my heeled shoes off and tip toe as quietly as possible, past the living room towards my room.

"Is that you Lisa?" The voice is familiar, but it's not Stevie's. I raise my head heavenwards and turn into the living room with a stomach full of dread.

"Hi Stubbsy, what's happening?" Stubbsy is lying flat out on the settee finishing off the wine I had opened earlier. It always amazes me how easily Stubbs can make himself look so at home in so many homes that aren't his own.

He looks me up and down, realizes that I've been crying, turns back to the TV and says, "Good date?" It's as if he knows, but I'm not going to give him the satisfaction.

"Eh yeah, not bad, not bad." As I say this, I can feel the tears running down my face. I look up at him pleadingly. I want him to hold me, hold me all night and keep me safe. But he doesn't. He picks up his jacket, swivels to his feet and says something that makes me feel violated once more.

"You know, cunts hate a cock-tease, hen. Ye sleber all over the guy at the Beer Festival, then show him the red card next time you're out. Can't blame the guy, really. See ye."

He leaves the flat with me howling the most painful of tears. I am left with a debilitating hatred for men, and one man in particular, and not the one who plays flute for the Netherton Orange Band.

CHAPTER 8

CASENOTES

CAROLYN AND LINDA MET FOR COFFEE EVERY WEDNESDAY AFTERNOON. Timetable wise it was the only time of the week they were both free. They had been friends since Uni, where they both studied Social Sciences. Carolyn stayed with the subject and eventually became a lecturer in Psychology. Linda used her honours degree to venture into the world of counselling and had become a highly respected cognitive therapist. Despite earning a decent living through her own surgery, Linda felt the urge to give something back. She became a full time Counselling Skills lecturer at Motherwell College in 2003. She enjoyed it. The students that came through her door were always eager to learn, and also eager to help. Some students were failed social workers who, due to bureaucratic intervention, had become disillusioned with their career choices and wanted to make a difference at a more personal level. Other students had received some sort of counselling themselves and felt they could pass on some of the experience of their therapy to others. Unfortunately, there were those, younger ones mainly, who were here simply as a means to an end. Putting off their entrance into the real world for as long they could.

Although she originally had hopes of working through at Jordon Hill College in Glasgow – closer to her flat in Shawlands and a far better college – the bonus of plying her trade in Motherwell was Carolyn. Her friend from Uni had done well. She had become principle Psychology lecturer after only three years. Two years later, she was made head of the Social Sciences Department. She wasn't popular, neither with staff nor pupils. She didn't suffer fools, but at the same time she never took anything personally: late essays, disagreements, insults, it was all part of the job. She was a strong one was Carolyn, and Linda loved her for that.

One of the many positive aspects of having a professional friend working in the same place as you is that you can seek them out and pick their brains on certain aspects of your job, and you know that the advice they offer will incorporate personal experiences that they know you will understand. They can relate certain incidents to situations that they know you have encountered. About three weeks ago, Linda asked Carolyn to read the case notes of a married couple she had been working with. If she was honest, she had hit a brick wall with them. Their marriage was in difficulty and the problem lay with the husband, but not in the conventional way most husbands let their wives down.

ALISTAIR

NAME: ALISTAIR BLANEY

OCCUPATION: ASSISTANT MANAGER MORRISONS SUPERMARKET WISHAW

AGE: 26

Alistair, on the face of it, comes across as a decent, hardworking, loving husband. The love he displays for his wife seems to border somewhat on the maternal. Throughout the course of our discussions, Alistair seems to feel a great need to prove himself to his wife, in the same way a son would seek the approval of a domineering mother, this despite the fact his wife doesn't seem to portray any such characteristics.

MARIE

NAME: MARIE BLANEY

OCUPATION: PRIMARY SCHOOL TEACHER

AGE: 27

Marie is a strong, opinionated individual who seems to have a much clearer definition of her and Alistair's marriage. Despite coming from what appears to be a solid loving background, Marie has an innate need to feel loved and wanted. She firmly believes that her husband's failure to satiate this need is the root of their marital problems.

ALISTAIR

FUTURE ACTION: Alistair must be encouraged to be more forceful when presenting his feelings and beliefs, and to know the importance of presenting HIS OWN feelings on certain subjects and not just ones which he thinks may placate his wife.

MARIE

FUTURE ACTION: Marie must seek the positives in her marriage and try and relate better to her husband's character. She must approach her husband with how she feels in a less combative manner and be patient with his responsiveness towards her.

Carolyn read Linda's case notes through and tried to picture the couple in question. Despite her professionalism, she couldn't help conjuring up images of Clark Kent and Louis Lane in the old Superman films.

"They seem quite a pair," Carolyn mused as she took off her reading glasses.

"Very modern."

"Really, in what way?" Linda asked.

"The domineering female. What on earth is happening to the male of the species!"

"It's weird though, Carolyn, you should see them. She looks amazing, you know, one of those girls who can wear long flowery dresses all the time, very little make-up, high bone structure? *She* is a beautiful – but him?" Linda laughed. "My God, he's this big beanpole with pale skin, sunken eyes and thin, almost jet-black hair. They are so mismatched it's almost laughable, but you know what, it's like she fancies him more than he does her!"

"How do you mean?" Linda enquired putting down her coffee cup and leaning forward, suddenly intrigued.

"Well, despite being absolutely besotted with her, he doesn't seem to find her attractive at all. I asked him to list the things he likes about her. He mentioned her character, her kindness, sense of humour, but not her obvious good looks."

"But she's attracted to him?"

"Totally, and she's very protective of him. I think she believes their problems lie in his low self-esteem. But I don't think it's that at all. He seems adequately self-assured about most things in his life. He just doesn't seem sure about how he feels about her."

"You don't think he's, well, gay?"

"Mmmm, ha! I never considered that! If he is he's doing a very good job repressing it. God, how am I going to approach this one?" Linda said to herself.

"With the diplomacy of a true professional," Carolyn exclaimed.

As the two friends made headway into their second round of coffees, the conversation turned to an individual whom they both had some insight into.

"So how did it go with my star pupil?" Carolyn asked.

"Oh, Mr Costello! It was interesting, though I made a bit of a booby!" Linda giggled into her coffee mug.

"What did you say, you mad bitch?" Carolyn laughed, remembering her friend's tendency for saying the wrong things at the wrong time.

"I called him 'Holden'!"

"You what?"

"I know, it's bad, I couldn't help it. He was going on about how much he hated Motherwell, all the people and their attitudes, and he was right, I agreed with everything he was saying, but it just came out. He saw the funny side though, thank God."

"I'm worried about him," Carolyn said, changing the tone of the conversation.

Linda rummaged through her briefcase and dug out the few notes she had written on Stevie.

"He's a troubled soul," she agreed.

"All through the wee session, I had one word was going through my head again and again, "lost". From his childhood right through his adolescence and up until the present day, he has had to adapt to those he loves most leaving him. His mother, father and girlfriend have all prematurely, and in some cases tragically, left his life. It's a credit to him that he has turned into the young man that he has. Any other young male I've come across who's had to deal with a similar situation has turned to crime or drugs, or both."

"Yes, but my fear is that he has the same anger and resentment as these individuals you talk about, but he is directing it at society on a more intellectual level. The fact of the matter is, he is channelling his anger towards a target that he knows won't fight back, when what he should be doing is exploring his feeling towards his parents and girlfriend."

Carolyn realized that what she had said had an angry tone to it that betrayed her usual composed way of interacting. She also knew that Linda knew, and that Linda would not let it go.

"Are you ok, Carolyn?"

"Linda, I can look out for the welfare of my students without some kind of hidden sexual agenda, if that's what you're implying."

"He is cute though," Linda said, raising her eyebrows.

"He needs help. He has a mind that would knock you for six Linda, honestly. The stuff he hands in has me perplexed. It's referenced from sources even I haven't heard of. I just don't think he's coping."

"He said he's not angry but disappointed. Not only with his situation, but with the world in general. Sometimes people who are as insightful and clever as Stevie are at a disadvantage compared to the rest of us, in that his intelligence means he can never be ignorant; he sees things other people don't see and, unfortunately, carries that weight on his shoulders," Linda said draining the last of her coffee.

The two friends carried on this topic for a while, occasionally changing to others. They weren't to know the link between both their clients, one of life's strange coincidences that would probably pass both of them by forever.

CHAPTER 9

SPRING DRINKS WITH STUBBS

IT'S GETTING NICE, MAN. NAE DOUBTS. I actually wouldn't have minded the wee walk tae the bus stop, but Alistair has insisted on giving me a lift. I'm meeting Stubbsy doon the Tav for a well-earned scoop. Alistair has to go over to the Hamilton shop and offered to drop me off.

"Ehm, Steve, would it be ok if we swung past mine, I have to pick something up," Alistair asks nervously, as if I'd somehow object because technically he would be doing so within working hours. The boy's crackers.

"Ahm sure ah can allow it this time," I say, looking at his face and hoping he realized I was joking.

"Thanks Steve, mate, I appreciate it." Fuckin hell!

After about five minutes' driving, we approach a cul-de-sac, which I assume is where Alistair lives. It's a nice conventional part of Wishaw that doesn't surprise. What does though is the person leaving the Fiat Uno on his driveway, carrying a handful of Asda shopping bags.

"Is that your wife, Alistair?"

"Yes, that's Marie, shopping in Asda again. I swear she does that just to annoy me."

The stories are true. She's gorgeous. Long, jet black hair tied back, showing off her beautiful face. She goes into the house then re-emerges with a document. Alistair obviously phoned her ahead, so as not to waste too much of Morrisons' precious time. How did she end up with him? She leans into the car unintentionally sending my loins into outer space. Tight black jeans show off the sexiest arse I think I've ever seen.

"This is Steve," Alastair says, closely scanning the piece of paper Marie passed to him.

"So you're Stevie. He doesn't stop going on about you. Just finished?"

"Eh aye, just loused." He introduced me as Steve, but she called me Stevie. Ahm liking this girl.

"So do you like it then, Safeway, oh sorry, Morrisons?" she laughs.

"Eh aye, it's been fine so far," I say, clearing my throat and trying not to catch this vision's eye.

"Ha, who you trying to kid? It's shite up there. I used to work there too, you know, that where I met laughing boy here." She nods her head towards Alastair who's got his head firmly stuck in the document in his hand and is totally oblivious to our conversation.

"Do they still take the piss out of him?" she asks making a funny face in his direction.

"Eh not that I am aware of," I lie.

"Just as well. You can be my eyes and ears up there, Stevie boy, look after him," she says with a wink. "What time can I expect you home tonight, my darling?" Marie says turning to her husband.

"Usual time I hope, love." He gives her an innocent look that she seems to know only too well.

Alastair drops me off at the Town Hall in Motherwell, and ah make my way up to the Tav. The sun on ma back blazes through my thin white shirt. Probably should have went up the Chopper, them havin the beer garden in that. When ah enter the pub, ah see big Stubbsy holding court with some auld drunkards who have probably been in here since openin' and have pished themselves about three times since then.

"Stevie, ma son! Best lookin hun in Motherwell, ha ha, ya cunt, whit's happenin?"

I take a seat to the grumbles of "Who's a hun?" fae the old guys. The Tav being Motherwell's premier Celtic shop. Stubbsy's pissed and being all matey. The old boys are lovin' it. He's probably pished and bought them all at least two drinks each.

"Whit's been happenin' big fella, you on it?" ah say pointing towards the gents' toilets.

"Na man, just this," he says holding up his poisonous looking pint of lager. "Ching's shite roond here the noo, anyway. The Airdrie boys of got the best gear supposedly." He goes and buys me a drink and we make our way to a table.

"Heard fae Lisa?" ah ask him. It's mental you can live wi' somebody but go for days without seeing them. She was out dating the other night, the wee minx. Ah love ma wee Lisa. Ah'll bell her later.

"Eh nah, man, fuck her, let's git blitzed."

The way the big man goes on aboot Lisa. Ah used think that maybe it was cause he secretly liked her. But lately, there's been a wee edge to his put-doons. Like there's bona fide resentment there, which is a bit childish, to be honest. We chew the fat for a bit about different things, the fitba and that. Ah start telling him about Alistair's wife, knowing how much he hates seeing good looking birds wi' glaykit looking guys.

"Honestly mate, ye want tae see this thing. Gorgeous, man. And him? Big fuckin daftie, you wouldn't believe it. School teacher tae, wirnae like that back in ma day!" ah says tae him, finishing off my Corona.

"Aye, fuckin tragedy. Tell ye whit though, bet she wisnae as tidy as the wee teacher I wis way last week. Mind last week in here, I ended up going back wi' a couple ah chickadees?"

"Aye, cannae mind what they looked like though," ah say, sookin another bottle ay Corona doon tae just the drowned, green lemon.

"Well, the one ah wis firin' intae wis no bad, nice figure and that, but her pal was well tidy, man. The thing was though, and don't ask me how it happened, ah ended up back at the tidy one's house sippin' away on the white wine. Thing wis though, she wisnae after some blond bomber action," Stubbsy says pointing tae eysel.

"How do ye mean?" ah says.

"Fuckin' weird, man. She just wanted me tae hing around till are man got back fae the backshift. Make um think thit there was something goin' on. Make um jealous, know what ah mean?"

"Whit? And ye done it? You're fuckin mental, by the way."

"The cunt was mair feart thin a wiz. Come ay think about it, ah should have joost shagged her, if eys gonnae think that anyway."

At this point, Gerry and Eddie come through the side door.

"Ahh right, ma son, whit's happening?" Stubbsy melodised tae Big Gerry, slappin' him round the back.

"Awrite, Eddie son, whit's the scandal?" ah says tae wee Eddie.

"Fack all, ma sunn, apart fae whit they're aboot tae serve me," Eddie says noddin' towards the bar. Wee Eddie's awrite man. If yer oan the boattles, instead ay the pints, he always buys ye two, which was good since ah wis faily firin' clean intae the old Corona.

"Fancy the toon, by the way?" Gerry says sippin his first ay the Guinness, gien himself a wee cream moustache. Ye could tell his suggestion that we head intae Glesga lit a few light bulbs.

"Aye man, that sound like a plan, by the way," Stubbs says, downing his pint impressively. "There's a Virgin express in ten, c'mon drink up."

We head round to the train station and get our ticket money out, as there's ticket collectors at the top of the stairs. Stubbsy just walks past them. The express train's the fuckin business, ten minutes and yer in, plus the bonus ay getting a swatch at the wee honey bees travelling up from London.

We hit a pretty conventional Irish pub on St Vincent Street. It's one seventy-five a pint of Guinness, outstanding for the town, so we start hammering intae the black stuff. Stubbs and Eddie are eying up a wee Greek looking barmaid who turns out to have the strongest Irish accent ah've ever heard. She has us all drooling over our pints when she drops an ice cube and skilfully flicks it into the bin with her left foot, Glen Hoddle style, much to all our amazement. It turns out she plays Gallic fitba, which is just like normal fitba on acid.

"Intae wee Irish sort, tae be sure," Stubbsy sais, puffin the chist out.

"Thought you were Al Green true love fir the wee Lisa one, ya cunt?" Big Gerry sais, winking my way aw cocky.

"We goat a fuckin hero here, Costello or whit?" Stubbsy sais, pure starin' nae-fuckin-jokes eyes at big Gerry, wide as fuck.

"Right girls, that's enough," ah say, trying ma best tae lighten the situation. Cunts and birds, some carry oan, ma son!

We head up tae the Suby for ah bit top class clubbing, but Wee Eddie gits knocked back for being oot it. We end up in some Glesgy shit tip. Nae drugs so wir soon oan the halves. Big Gerry starts firing intae this big fat thing next tae the lassies' toilet, leaving the rest of us in a dark corner of the hideous night spot. It's all neon and smoke, you can see the dandruff on the guy's shoulders and the birds that irnae wearing underwear. Whit a place. Am just aboot tae suggest that we go to get a kebab or something when Stubbsy grabs my arm.

"Whit's wrang?" ah ask him.

"Cunts," he sais, lookin' straight in my eye.

"Who? Whit ye on aboot, ay?"

"They bastards, they aw fuckin' left ye, that daft bird, yer maw and da, who the fuck dae they think they were ay?"

"C'mon big man, you're melted, ahm fine man," ah say, tryin' tae calm the situation.

"Yer no bit, mate, ah can tell, your no fine, ah've been watching ye man, staring intae space aw the time. THAT WEE BURD WIS A SELFISH COW FUR WHIT SHE DID, LEAVIN YOU LIKE THAT, NO FUCKIN RIGHT, BY THE WAY!" he sais wiping away the tears of frustration from his eyes. Am dumbfounded. Ah don't think ah've ever seen him like this. It's shocked us man.

"C'mon son, it's cool, lets git the other two, head up George square for a fast wan." As ahm saying this he gently turns me round by the arm so he can look me right in the eye.

"Ah'll never leave ye, ma son. Ye fuckin hear that? Never. No the way they did. Ah've no been right lately, things in ma heid ah've had tae work out for masel. Not noo though, ah can see everything and every cunt for what they really are. You're never going ay be oan yer own as long as ahm aboot, right?" He pulls me towards him and ah find masel startin' to well up a bit, but ah fight it. Nae room for tears in this soldier make up.

The journey home is a sombre one. Gerry and Eddie, realising something heavy had gone down between me and the big fella, sensibly decide not to probe. Stubbsy sits in the front seat no saying a word.

We didn't know it then, but tonight would be his last night out as a single man.

CHAPTER 10

UNDER A MOTHERWELL SUN

THE GOOD PEOPLE OF MOTHERWELL HADN'T SEEN ANYTHING quite like it in a long, long time. Bright, beautiful sunshine splashed between the dark brown seventies style buildings that racked up in every street between Strathclyde Park and Wishaw General. Those of a more malted skin texture lapped up the unexpected change in temperature, topping up tans from past glories of Glasgow fairs gone by. Some of a fairer skin type exposed themselves with a defiance that was almost Churchillian. "Let this shining fireball do it's very worst," you could almost hear them say, "we shan't bow to its might!" And then there were those of a certain hair colour, stalking in the shadows, silently wishing that the rain and natural greyness of this old steel town would return sooner rather than later.

Stubbsy turned round in alarm, letting the silver tubing he was bending fall to the floor. Wee Ryan Farrell, one of the first-year apprentices just recently started with the electrical firm Stubbsy worked for, came running breathlessly towards him with a look of panic in his young boyish face. Behind him was Mark 'Porky' O'Rourke, a newly qualified spark. Behind him, Tam Feelan, a third-year apprentice from East Kilbride who had an appalling reputation for treatment of first-year boys.

"Problem boys?" Stubbs asked, clocking the tin of paint in Tam's hand.

"Och, nothin', Stubbs mate, joost fuckin aboot, Friday in that," Porky said nervously turning to walk away.

"Fuck that, initiate the cunt, boy's getting painted!" Tam shouted, making a lunge for the young apprentice. Stubbs stood himself in front of Ryan.

"Whit's your name again son?" Stubbsy asked Tam dismissively.

"Tam Feelan, how?" Tam replied as gallous as he could, although there was a slight hint of trepidation in his voice. He'd never worked on a job with Stubbsy before, although he had heard all about him. His mauling of a bouncer at the Motherwell Beer Festival was now stamped in Lanarkshire folklore. No sooner had Stubbsy wiped the blood from his fists, than the story was reverberating around the streets of Wishaw, Bellshill, Hamilton and East Kilbride.

"Well, Tam Feelan-How, this is whit's going to happen. Wee Ryan here going ay help me cut this tubing tae size and put it up because, Friday or no, we've got a fuckin job tae finish here. You and yer boyfriend are going tae fuck off out my face and hope that ah don't hear about you terrorising any mair boys, on this job or any other job, cause see if ah dae, ah'll no be painting yer baws, ah'll be kickin them up and down the fuckin joab, goat it?"

"Aye, sound, Stubbsy mate, nae hassle," Porky said pushing Tam in the opposite direction. Ryan watched his tormentors sheepishly walk back to the work hut, breathing a sigh of relief. He felt safe in the knowledge that he had managed to survive another week with his balls still the same colour.

"Right you, hold this, an keep it fuckin straight," Stubbsy said slapping the back of Ryan's head. The apprentice grabbed the steel conduit and held it firmly against the wall in line with the chalk mark, all the time looking at the big blond workhorse beside him, wishing every spark was as decent as him.

The sun was strong on the back of Stubbsy's neck as he walked up Bellshill Road. He decided to let more than one bus pass him by. A day as beautiful as today had to be enjoyed, so he made the decision to walk to his next destination. As he paced slowly through Brandon Parade the old song by Paddy Reilly, 'The Town I Loved So Well', came into his head. Stubbsy loved Motherwell. Loved the people, loved the atmosphere. He couldn't ever see himself living anywhere else. He liked the odd night in Glasgow like everyone else, but he could never see himself living there. His rose tinted view of his hometown was completely at odds to that of his best friend. Stevie hated Motherwell and was continually running the place down. Stubbsy had to admit that most of it was justified. He was a clever guy, Stevie, and had a canny habit of putting an opinion across so intelligently that even if you totally disagreed with what he said, you couldn't help find yourself agreeing with him at some kind of level.

The one thing that Stubbsy could never agree with Stevie on was the idea that happiness could only be achieved with moving out of Motherwell and Scotland entirely. This, according to Stubbsy, was pure garbage. He had seen so many friends and family selling up everything they own and moving away to Canada or Australia, countries some of them had never even been to in their life! Stubbsy could accept that the change of temperature and culture would, for a little while at least, be enjoyable. But after a time, once the novelty had worn off, surely life, and all the things that come with it, would be exactly the same. You still get council tax in Australia. Credit card bills in Canada, parking tickets, late trains and buses. Crap beer, crap food, bank charges, politicians and Mormons. They're still there, in South Africa, America, or whichever destination is the place to be this week. According to Stubbsy, it didn't matter where you went; Monday mornings would still be shite and Friday nights would still be rockin! No arguments.

As he walked past Starka, the idea of slipping in for an ice cold Stella became almost overwhelming, but he marched on knowing that, despite the beautiful weather and the fact it was the start of the weekend, Stubbsy had to stay focused. What he was about to do required him to keep his wits about him.

Instead of walking up Windmill Hill Street, which was busy and congested, he opted to walk through Orbison Street, which was adjacent to the road he was on. If anyone ever asked Stubbsy to show him a place that summed up what Motherwell was all about, Stubbsy would take them to Orbiston Street. It was quiet yet industrious. "Just like the people of Motherwell," Stubbsy thought, pleased that he had made a simile that showed his town folk in a positive light for a change. It was a street that was lined with small, reasonably successfully businesses that managed to buck any prevailing economic up or downturn and solidly provided the town with services and employment it so badly needed. He passed by joiner shops, card factories, frame designers and a bright green building that had been there for as long as Stubbsy could remember, but hadn't a clue what it was. These little entrepreneurial schemes were perpetrated by normal tradesmen and stockists. In the grand scheme of things they were all relatively new businesses; few of them had been handed down from previous generations and there was certainly no big high street conglomerates here. Just normal folk who had made the most of cash windfalls they came into, inheritance, redundancy etc. It was one of the true shining examples of the Britain that Margaret Thatcher envisaged when she set about destroying the mining villages and steel towns of old. The fact that Orbiston Street was the spine of Scotland's third safest Labour stronghold was an irony not lost on even Stubbsy's untrained political mind.

The flats in Muirhouse acted as an unsteady handshake between Motherwell and Wishaw. Stubbsy approached the third tower that jutted over the surrounding maisonettes and into the clear blue sky like an awkward child at playschool, taller and clumsier than his fellow play pals. Stubbsy didn't have to wait long at the secure entrance as a delivery driver with bags full of Scottish cuisine held the door open for him. The congealed calorie buster in those bags was being enjoyed, no doubt, up and down the land and working wonders for the country's population control. When Stubbs reached the eighth floor, he took a deep breath and walked towards door number forty-six. He chapped the door and waited. Waited and waited. No answer. Stubbsy was about to turn and leave when he heard a fumble of the chain and the turn of a key. He put one foot in front of the other and clenched his fists. The door opened and a dumpy young girl wearing a Motherwell strip stared blankly at him.

"He's no in, away the saunas," she said turning away and closing the door.

"Aquatec?" Stubbsy asked hopefully.

"Sports Centre," she replied slamming the door shut.

Stubbsy stood on the landing staring out the window towards Craignuek, the direction the Sports Centre was. After a few minutes deliberating, he decided to head up towards Wishaw Sports Centre. It was a couple of miles away and, as lovely as it was outside, Stubbs didn't fancy the walk and a stuffy bus journey at going home time was out of the question. He decided on a cab. The weather being as it was, he didn't have to wait long for a taxi. The driver initially tried some small talk, but gave up once he realized Stubbs wasn't interested.

It wasn't until he arrived at the Sports Centre that Stubbs realized that the last time he was here they didn't have a swimming pool let alone a sauna. Stubbsy wasn't into all that health spa shite; in fact, he was trying to work out what a sauna was – the hot sweaty place or the bubbly bath thing? He entered the building and walked straight through the reception with the confidence of a card carrying member, which thankfully raised no suspicion. He walked through the changing rooms and into the swimming area where the sauna was. He stopped at the side of the pool, recognizing a life guard who looked at him: first with bemusement, but this turned to abject horror as he realized what was going down. This would be one shift the swimming attendant would not forget.

Robbie Peters was not a happy bunny. It was his third Friday in a row he had worked. He knew the reason of course. Everyone in the Sports Centre knew he'd started dating Becky Stapleton from the gym and that she always worked on a Sunday morning, which meant Friday was the only decent chance they had of a night out together. Dean Nolan, the pool supervisor, knew this and took great pleasure in sticking him on the backshift, no doubt in the ridiculously vain hope that he could make a move on her. She'd be down Starka tonight with her friends and he would be there, on his own, leering over her at every opportunity. He trusted Becky. Loved her, in fact. They were going through that sweet honeymoon period, where it feels like there's no one else on earth, where you seem to see the best in everything and everybody. What kind of saddo goes into a pub like Starka on his own on a Friday night? As if that wasn't enough, he had the displeasure of Fraser Douglas, who had come into use the sauna, slavering in his ear. Robbie hated Fraser. He played in the same flute band as his big brother and thought this gave him the right to talk to him like he was *his* younger brother. Plus, he despised his constant vulgar barrage involving any female in the vicinity. Fraser was a truly horrible individual and Robbie wouldn't be surprised if the rumours about what he'd done with that lassie outside Mega bar were true.

Just as he was about to go on his tea break, Robbie noticed something out of the corner of his eye that, at first, confused him, then, as he began to work out what was going on, scared him so much that he almost blew his whistle instinctively. A large, imposing, fully-clothed figure with short blond hair and big blue eyes walked steadily around the perimeter of the pool, past the chill out area and towards the sauna room. The sauna room where Fraser was.

Robbie knew the individual only as Stubbs or Stubbsy and that he was not to be messed with, something Robbie had quickly decided was not worth the minimum wage he was earning. He also knew that this feller was best mates with that guy from Motherwell whose girlfriend had killed herself and, what's more, that he shared a flat with the girl that Fraser was supposed to have mauled a few weeks back. Robbie did the sums and realised that, although tonight was a shift he didn't want to do, it was one he would remember for a very long time.

Fraser Douglas felt his pores open up and the sweat run down his pot belly, making him feel both flustered and invigorated. He preferred the Sports Centre over the Aquatec, even though the Aquatec was closer. He enjoyed watching the young girls who came from St Aiden's High in with their swimsuits, their bodies not quite yet formed, young enough to be manipulated into doing whatever he wanted. He also knew that he was better off doing his thing in Wishaw, as opposed to Motherwell these days. His date with that Lisa hadn't been a roaring success. He could have behaved better, he conceded. But she was a teasing cow; she had led him on, up dancing with him, then giving him the cold shoulder. Who the fuck did she think she was? If she had just let him shag her. She wouldn't be all depressed (he had heard that she hadn't been across the door since that night, but had so far, thankfully, not told anyone what had really happened). He decided to keep his head down for a bit just in case, wait for things to calm down, then go with the flow. If anyone asked he would say that she was well up for it, but he knocked her back; let people think she was the skank he knew she really was.

The hot, steaming conditions and the thought of seeing the young schoolies in the adjacent changing rooms were enough to give him a healthy erection. "The sauna's empty," he thought. He could whip out his cock right now and have a chug on the fly. No, he would wait till he was safely home, with his laptop. Slutty babysitters was a current favourite. He closed his eyes and rubbed the sweat away from his face. As he did this, he could hear the door of the sauna creaking open, the incoming gush of cool air a welcoming refreshment. He opened his eyes and squinted at the sight that was before him – confused, he wiped his eyes once more.

"Awrite, lover boy," the guy standing in front of him said. At first he thought it was one of the pool attendants, because he was fully clothed. Another look told him that this was no employee of Wishaw Sports Centre. The black, cuffed, size eleven steelies, the blue overalls tied at the waist, and the blond hair. It was the hair that told Fraser that everything was not all right and he was in big trouble.

"Stubbsy, man, whit's happening?" he asked, nervously watching the door and praying someone would come in.

Stubbsy swivelled a clear uppercut, which caught Fraser squarely on the mouth, loosening a couple of teeth and filling his mouth with acidic, red blood. Stubbsy grabbed him by the hair and smashed his jaw firmly against the hard edge of the clear tiled seats, breaking it instantly.

"Awww, Stubbsy, please, please man, ma, ma, face please."

Stubbsy was sweating more than he had ever done before and knew that if anyone came in the sauna at this point, he would be done for. Looking about a room that was strange to him, he realised that there was nothing he could get his hands on so any more damage would have to be done with his bare hands. But it was so warm and he felt his energy levels failing. He grabbed Fraser's torso, which was slippery with blood and sweat. He opened his left eye and plunged his thumb straight into the socket and held it for as long as he could. Fraser let out another sickening cry as he felt his full eye pop from its socket. It was a pain he had never experienced and thought, and hoped, he would pass out.

"Never met a real rapist before," Stubbsy said breathlessly, sweat lashing from his head.

"Am no' a, ah never... arghh."

Stubbsy slammed the sole of his boot into Fraser's groin, clocking a wooden spoon next to some hot coals.

"You're a fuckin beast and ye beasted a pal ay mines, don't fuckin deny it. Ah've got my spies, a taxi driver ah know saw ye trying it on wi her up the close, and her trying ay get away."

The sweat, especially in his jeans under his overall, was now overwhelming and building up like a dam. Stubbsy grabbed Fraser's trunks and pulled them off, Fraser groaning, but in too much pain to do anything about it. Taking off his overalls and using them to protect his hand, Stubbsy picked up the wooden bucket of fiery, hot coals. Kicking Fraser on to his front where his limp cock was exposed, Stubbsy emptied the burning embers on to Fraser's front, scalding the skin of penis and balls so much that his innards began to seep from his ballsack area, the sickening smell of burning flesh becoming overpowering. Fraser squealed, this time loud enough for others in the swimming area to hear. Stubbsy took this as his cue to leave. As he departed to funny looks from the rest of the swimmers, he walked past the swimming attendant and raised an eyebrow as if to say, "You've seen nothing."

Once outside, Stubbsy discarded his charred overalls and made his way back to Motherwell, this time jumping on a 240 bus that was passing. Before heading home, he went into the Dalziel Arms for a pint. Although his sweat from before had almost dried up, the lack of fluids in his body had left him with a killer thirst. He ordered a bottle of water, went out to the beer garden and downed it in one, then proceeded to drink his pint slowly. He thought about what he had done. Did he go over the top? Probably, but he had to teach him a lesson. Stubbsy hoped that the next time he thought about treating a woman so disgustingly, Fraser would feel the burns marks on his dick, balls and thighs and think again. Was he worried about comebacks? From Fraser, no. He had no connection other than the divs he played with in the Orange band, none of who caused him any concern. Cops? Maybe. He was sure they would be at the Sports Centre now taking statements, along with an ambulance, no doubt. He was confident Fraser wouldn't mention his name, through fear if anything else. That only left the swimming attendant. Stubbsy recognised him, but didn't know him well enough to rely on his discretion. And even though it was his word against Stubbs's, he knew he'd have to be careful.

The sun was beginning to lose its ferocity as the afternoon turned to evening, leaving a fresh mildness that was far more suited to the Scottish taste. The cold, fizzy lager slid down his throat, relaxing his mind and body. He thought about Stevie, his best mate and what he'd been through. He thought about Motherwell, the town he loved so well, and how beautiful a place it was to be when the sun was shining. And as he emptied his glass and motioned to the bar maid, who had come out to collect glasses, to set him up another, he thought about the real reason why he'd done what he'd done. Under this fine Motherwell sun he dropped the bravado that had characterised his whole being so far. Because it was only now, after such ugly actions in such an uplifting climate, that he could finally admit the feeling he had for a long time now. For the first time in his life, Gary Stubbs was in love.

CHAPTER 11

CLARE'S THE ANGEL I HAD IN MY EYE

MY ADMIRATION AND RESPECT FOR JACK MURRAY STRETCHED much further than the usual false-laugh-at-everything-he-says-because-he's-your-girlfriend's-dad affair. Jack was, in the truest sense of the word, a political heavy-weight. He managed to somehow intricate the most radical of New Labour initiatives from the most draconian of left wing ideologies and was used ruthlessly by the Labour hierarchy to sell it to the unconvinced masses.

When I began dating his daughter, I found myself constantly asking about him. Clare found this amusing at first, but eventually grew tired of my constant inquisitions and introduced us properly. I can remember the first night we met. Clare and I had arranged to go to the Floorshaker in the Electric Bar. After two hours of putting the world to rights with her father, poor Clare decided to leave us to it and left for the Floorshaker on her own. I never even realised she was gone.

Jack was a warm, personable man. He made whoever he was talking to, whether it be a council chief or an everyday constituent, feel like they were the most important person in the world. Our friendship grew and eventually he invited me to join his small 'Impact Team'. This was a collection of people who dedicated their lives and time to the Labour Party. At first, I was surprised that such groups existed. I always thought the people who worked on a political candidate's election campaigns did so only on the time leading up to an election. But the impact team spent every day of their lives trying to work out plans and implementations that would eventually lead to a Labour victory in any forthcoming elections. It was hard work – tedious and boring – and I loved every minute of it. Whenever you felt like you were hitting a brick wall and doors were literally being slammed in your face, the thought that you were doing it for Jack made it all worthwhile.

The strength of the political ideal that I shared with Jack pales into insignificance compared to the tie that binds us now.

Clare went missing on Friday the sixth of September. She had arranged to meet a friend for coffee in Hamilton, but hadn't turned up. By eleven o'clock that night she was still posted as missing and everyone who knew Clare began to worry about how out of character this was. Usually, the police give it a few days before investigating the disappearance of an adult, but in Clare's case, given the high profile of her father, they began searching for her almost immediately.

On a personal level I felt completely numb. To be honest, I was sure she was dead by lunchtime the following day. Like I said, for Clare not to turn up for a pre-arranged meeting, to not get in touch, it was all way out of character. After a few days, the search for her went nationwide with Jack doing a press conference, where he desperately pleaded with his daughter to come home. The police were now moving towards the notion that Clare had somehow come to harm. This meant me being interrogated about the nature of my relationship with her by local C.I.D. officers. To be fair, they didn't lean too hard. At first, when I told them that we had split – amicably, I might add – a few weeks before, they became slightly suspicious. I'm no crime expert, but I would figure this would be enough to put me in the frame if anything had happened to her. They eased off, however, when I told them I had been in Stirling with Clare's dad and the rest of the impact team that night, and almost thirty different people had seen or spoken to her since I last did.

A week had passed when the news we all dreaded, but by now morbidly expected, arrived. Police had found Clare's car at the edge of a high cliff off the Lead Hills, which overlooked deep waters that headed out towards the Irish Sea. In it were some loose possessions including her phone, handbag and a note; a suicide note, addressed to me.

Dear Stevie,

You always said that suicide was for the brave, so I'll address this to you in the hope that you, more than anyone, will understand. I am dead now Stevie. I stood up to the sadness, like you always said I should. Your theory, remember? Why? Why am I ending my life? Well, I don't want to get into the mechanics of it, not now and obviously not ever, it's not your problem Stevie. I have lived a not bad life and I should, by all reckoning, be in heaven by now, looking down on my Stevie, the one who could have been THE ONE. I said I didn't love you. But I did, not in a boyfriend way, or a brother way or even a friend way. Sometimes I would look into your big brown eyes and think I could see your soul, but I could never get there. Since the day we met I knew I was going to take my life. I never knew how, but always knew why. You opened me up to the notion of death Stevie, that it wasn't a bad thing, that taking your life wasn't the coward's way. I don't know how this will make you feel, and of course that's the problem. No one ever knows how you feel (as I write this there is a small part of me hoping this letter will elicit some kind of response from you, anger, hatred, resentment, but I'm not banking on it). You're a special boy Stevie, and if heaven is all the things you can ever wish for, I hope I can now watch your life from afar, watch you grow, to learn to live and to love and to once and for all find the happiness and peace of mind you so desperately want and so richly deserve.

Clare

And that was it. No explanation, no reason; just gone, just dead. The numbness prevailed for weeks after this. I couldn't be sad or angry, and I still don't know why this is the case. Rumours of why Clare had taken her life began to circulate furiously. The fact that she hadn't specified any particular reason meant that any story, no matter how ridiculous, could not be discounted. The usual suspects were put forward: debt, depression, pressure of living in her father's shadow. I can't dismiss any of these notions but I find them all rather tiresome.

One of the strangest theories doing the rounds was that Clare had staged the whole thing and was, in fact, still alive. *The Sun* ran a story that she had copied her 'idol' Richey Edwards from the 'Manic Street Preachers', who also left his car and a note at a well-known suicide spot and his body has never been recovered. This, in part, was a load of nonsense. Clare enjoyed listening to music, but wasn't especially passionate about any particular artist. She did actually own a Manics album but it was *This is My Truth Tell Me Yours*, the most un-Richey Edwards album they ever recorded; I would be surprised if she even knew who he was. This theory was eventually put to bed altogether when a body was washed up three miles from where Clare's car had been found. Jack had the horrible task of attending a post-mortem to identify his daughter. It was her.

The funeral was a sad, yet tense, affair. I haven't been to many and always find them stiflingly uncomfortable. I never know what to say, or not say, to a grieving family. This feeling of awkwardness was multiplied by ten at Clare's funeral when I was the one on the end of the sympathetic nods and small talk. I never cried or even felt like crying. All the time I could feel the eyes of everyone on me. Waiting for me to crack, to explode with emotion, in the hope they could gain some sense of proportion about the extent of this tragedy.

I didn't leave the house for days after the funeral. Part of me wanted to let the dust settle, but another part just wanted to get back out and get on with life. Stubbsy and Lisa were great and were on hand making sure I was ok. Eddie and Gerry came round once for an obligatory visit. Apart from them though, the first person I saw was Jack. I phoned ahead and he told me he was in the office and to come round and see him. When I arrived, Jack was on his own. It was strange seeing the office so quiet and isolated. It was usually a hive of activity and debate, but today it seemed tired and limp.

"Sit down, son," Jack said, pointing to an empty chair opposite his desk.

"Drink?" Jack wasn't a drinker – well he was a drinker, but not a bottle-of-whiskey-in-the-afternoon-in-his-office drinker.

"No thanks. How you keeping?" I asked, noticing the rings round his eyes and loosened tie which betrayed his normal sharp appearance. He looked tired.

"Och you know, bearing up. Mary's in an affy state, staring into space one minute, crying her eyes out the next."

"Ah can imagine." I couldn't actually. I could never imagine what it was like losing a child, but I was getting used to the post-funeral things-that-people-say.

"Jack, can ah ask you something?" I asked.

"Course you can, son," Jack said, knocking back a straight whiskey and wincing at its coarse texture.

"Why do you think she did it, Clare, ah mean, why do you think she killed herself?"

Jack stared into space for a minute, as if he was, strangely, contemplating this for the first time.

"When these things happen, Steven," he said, addressing me with a name that none except my own father uses, "the parents of the kids involved usually experience a helpless feeling of having not really known their offspring. Ah know this because ah've had constituents come to me many times and tell me they thought their kids were normal rounded individuals, only to find they were, in fact, drug dealers, drug addicts, BNP racists or even closet Tories!" He gave a little smile and shook his head to let me know he was joking, that he still had the ability to elicit good humour. That was one of Jack's major attributes.

"But with Clare," he said, suddenly becoming more serious, "ah always knew, perhaps in no more than a subconscious way, that she would do something like this. Since she was a little girl she was never afraid of anything. No matter what she was faced with, Clare would do whatever she wanted to do and, significantly, ah think, if there was something she couldn't or didn't want to do she would destroy it. Let me give you an example, Steven. When Clare was little, we bought her a big kid's jigsaw for her to play with. Ah left her in her room to play on her own. When I checked on her she was gone. Ah finally found her in the garden with a box of Mary's matches, trying to burn the jigsaw. When ah asked her why, she said it was because she couldn't do it, therefore she didn't need it in her wee life."

Jack leaned over towards me and took my hand in his, a gesture that didn't feel in the slightest bit uncomfortable. "She's gone, Steven, son, don't torture yourself with the hows and whys. Ah want you to move on, Steven. Ah need you here with me. Ahm not getting any younger and ah have to start thinking about the future of the Labour Party in Wishaw and Motherwell. It's abundantly clear to me and the Impact Team that you are that future, Steven, if you want it. Study Politics, son, get your degree and carry on the positive work ah've started."

I smiled bashfully, for the first time feeling awkward. I felt a wave of excitement come over me. For the first time in my life, I had a genuine purpose, and a clear map to follow. I had already applied to study Political Theory at Strathclyde University. Now I had a genuine reason to do it.

"Thanks, Jack, ah'll try not to let you down, man."

CHAPTER 12

STUBBS N' LISA: A MOTHERWELL LOVE STORY (PART ONE)

THE TOWN OF HAMILTON HAD, historically, always silently enjoyed a smug air of respectability that its more urban neighbours could never quite achieve. The Duke of Hamilton and his descendants, for instance, had dwelling rights here; rights that gave them status and power, passed down to them from ruling monarchs from a time that allowed them to accrue land and grand homes of decadent stature. Yes, East Kilbride had managed to drag itself from the embarrassing stereotype of Eighties New Town into an impressive plateau of modern-day shopping and family-friendly, do-everything-you-need-to-do-and-do-it-in-one-day type experience. But sadly, Motherwell and Bellshill still seemed to wallow in a self-defeating pity and had changed very little from the industrial boom of the sixties. Hamilton Academicals Football Club's new stadium, which would facilitate office space for new businesses and corporate functions, was the latest addition to the town's ever expanding commercial landscape.

Stubbsy wasn't happy. He wasn't being himself. In the last week or so, he had found himself doing things he would never do. What on earth was happening to him? It was Friday afternoon, in the new Douglas Park job. Ryan Farrell, the apprentice he had taken from the Chunghwa job a few weeks earlier, was hopping from foot to foot trying to hold the extended spirit level on the newly cut tray so that Stubbs could get a measure of its equilibrium. He daren't ask him what the holdup was, both out of fear and respect. It had only been a fortnight ago Stubbsy had saved him from the thuggish Porky O'Rourke and his can of paint. But now his arms were becoming heavy and he feared he might drop the krypton-like instrument altogether.

"Eh Stubbs man, ma arms, fuckin killin us mate, have ye got it level yet?" Ryan asked nervously, noticing Stubbs looking aimlessly towards Peacock Cross. He was staring wistfully towards a young couple who were holding the hands of a child, playing "one-two-weeee" with the kid who was loving every minute of it. He had an unfamiliar look of longing, a look Ryan had never seen before. It betrayed his usual allure that normally alternated between the cocksure and aggressive.

"Stubbs, the spirit level, ye got it or whit?" Ryan groaned. At this Stubbsy zapped back into life and glared at his young electrical protégé.

"Aye ah've fuckin well got it, ya cheeky wee cunt! Right, here away doon the van and git us two rolls in bacon, nae sauce mind, git yersel yer lunch ah naw and keep the change," Stubbsy said, throwing the boy a crisp purple twenty.

On the way down to the van, which sat next to the ever-expanding Bell College, Ryan did a quick tally of the weekend funds. His ma had given him a fiver to get to work, plus a couple of pounds for his lunch. Stubbsy always picked him up at the end of his street and dropped him at the New Century, a ten minute walk from his house. Once he had bought Stubbsy his lunch, a roll for himself, pocketed the skin, plus his mam's money, his meager weekly wage would be boosted by at least a quarter. Tonight, he would hit The Edge. This had to be his night with that wee Jade who works in Marcantonio's chip shop. Stubbs always used to tease him on a Monday morning after another heartbreakingly fruitless weekend chasing the elusive Jade in the usual trail of Starka, The Edge, then a dead-end party. A trail which inevitably led young huntsman Farrell to the home of his parents, to the bed they provided, on his own.

"No shagged that wee hing fae the Chippie yet, son?" Stubbs would not so much ask, than announce. "Honest tae God, man, see when ah was your age, ah hud tae pit oan Goldberg's own make ay aftershave just tae keep the young things away fae me! Didnae work right enough!" he would say in his usual jovial manner. This morning it was different though. On the way to the job he looked at Ryan as he fiddled with his mobile; he was checking how much charge he had, having forgotten to plug the charger in before he went to bed.

"Who was that? Was it Jade?" Stubbs asked, in a tone that was warmer than normal. It was also the first time he had called her by her first name.

"Eh naw, just checking ah've enough joos in the moby in case embday phones me, no," Ryan waited for the usual Stubbsy onslaught, which would mean the current status of his virginity, the size of his manhood and his overall masculinity being called into question. But it wasn't forthcoming.

"You should ask her out, Ryan, if you really like her, that is," Stubbsy said nodding towards Ryan's phone.

"Eh aye mibbe, see how it goes." Ryan never felt embarrassed by Stubbs's ritualistic onslaught of abuse, knowing as he did that it was always in jest, but this new expression of tenderness coming from his older sidekick had him blushing furiously.

After lunch, they did a half-hearted Friday afternoon's work and eventually packed up the tools and loaded the van just before three o'clock. As Stubbsy waved Ryan off at the New Century Bar on Windmill Hill Street, he reflected on the week that had gone by. Ryan was a nervous wee kid, but

Stubbsy knew that he was probably a little taken aback by his own behaviour. He was changing and he couldn't seem to help it. Last week he went to visit his mam, Jean, just for a catch up. It was Wednesday, the day his dad went to the bowling club, which meant his mum could get all her housework done. She loved nothing better, once the hoovering and polishing was complete, to stick on her Neil Sedaka LP and leisurely do the ironing. This had been a ritual she had stuck by since Stubbsy was a kid and the sound of this bland, cheesy music would normally send him round the bend, but on this occasion it was different. As Jean nattered away about all the babies that had been born and the people who had died, Stubbsy felt himself being drawn to the easy listening overtones emanating from the old stereo in the corner of the living room.

He felt a warm, mushy feeling in his stomach. The thick, homemade broth his mum had made would easily have been devoured, but now he couldn't face it. He couldn't face anything; he could only think of one thing, one person, one girl.

Lisa listened to the music with as much enthusiasm as she could muster, but, to her, the CD that Stevie had been raving about for a while now sounded pretty similar to all the other stuff he listened to. A wee bit like the guy from The Verve or REM, she wasn't really sure. They were called The Witness or The Witnesses or something. She was just happy that

Stevie was beginning to get back into his music again. She had noticed a change in him lately. He was the toast of the Motherwell College Social Sciences department for being the first student to be accepted into Strathclyde University to study Political Theory. He was chattier and even went to a work's night out with the folk from Morrisons. He'd hated it, but the fact he went was a bonus.

Lisa, on the other hand, was miserable. She looked in the mirror and noticed that her usually blonde shiny hair looked limp and greasy. A spot above her lip had decided to reside there permanently and her usual healthy size 10 figure was now somewhere nearer an 8. If this had been down to a diet or healthy living regime, she would have been delighted, but she knew the real reason was that she hadn't been eating properly; she just didn't have the appetite anymore. Things had been getting on top of her lately. Her first year at college was coming to an end, which meant a mad dash to get all her essays in. Her meeting with her real dad hadn't gone as well she would have hoped. He seemed ok, but hadn't been in touch for a while, which should have bothered her but didn't. Her social life had also hit a brick wall ever since the night she went on a date with that creep who tried to rape her. The fact she was able fight him off and give him a sore eye in the process gave her some comfort. She had also heard a rumour that he had been on the end of a serious beating and was walking with crutches, which would serve the creep right, but she also knew what Motherwell was like for rumours.

But the thing that was getting her down most was *him*. From the moment she met Stubbsy, she fancied him. He was her type; big, loud, totally full of himself, but warm, friendly and loyal too. They had their moments to start with. When Stevie first introduced them, Stubbs was flirty and full on. She loved it but knew the worst thing to do with guys like that was to capitulate too easily, as they tended to get bored if you did that. There was a brief period of cat and mouse that was fun, but when the whole Clare thing happened, he changed. It was like he began to see her as an enemy.

The way Lisa saw it was that they, as Stevie's best friends, should have stuck together to try and help him through such a difficult time. Stubbsy though, he seemed to turn it into an almost ridiculous paternity battle, like he wanted Stevie to himself. That's when the insults started. It was little digs at first, and then no-holds-barred insults. Lisa's hatred for him grew by the day, to the point she would lie in bed at night and wish the very worst to happen to him. There were times though, when she couldn't help herself. That night in the Beer Festival, she hadn't stopped thinking about what he did and why he did it. She thought about his sometimes unbelievable acts of generosity and the fact that whenever she was with him, in company or not, she always felt safe. She was in love with him, always had been, and that was the real reason she hated him so much.

Stubbsy lifted one arm, then the other, and shook his head in disbelief. Sweat patches? Under the armpits? What the fuck was going on with him? Standing outside Stevie's flat he took a deep breath. He knew Stevie wasn't in, but was about to pretend that he thought he was. He cleared his throat and knocked on the door. Knocked on the door? He had never knocked on the door in his life; this was getting too weird.

Lisa answered the door and looked at him quizzically. Stubbsy thought she looked tired and had lost some weight, but it couldn't camouflage her natural sexiness that seemed to ooze from her every pore. The blue eyes, hiding under that blonde fringe, and the way she always pushed her left hip to the side, pressing against her jeans when she spoke, it always turned Stubbsy on at some level. No, it was making his stomach do back flips.

"Stevie's not in," she said coldly, turning to go back in, then turning back. "Why did you knock, Stubbsy? You never knock."

"Eh pah... Don't know, man, just eh ehm, what's ehm, when's, wh... Stevie... eh can ah come in?" Stubbsy was stuttering like a fourteen year old being babysat by Angelina Jolie, but he couldn't help it. His throat was dry and he had never felt so nervous in his whole life.

"Can you come in? Are you asking me if you can come in? Of course you can," Lisa sneered. What was going on here? Was this one of his cruel wind ups, the chapping the door, the asking if he could stay, the wee shy boy routine. She hoped it wasn't; she didn't have the energy for it today.

"Ahm going to my room so make yourself at home," she said sarcastically, knowing full well that making himself at home was what Stubbsy did best.

"Eh thanks, ehm Lisa, eh… can ah have a word?"

Lisa looked at Stubbsy in the eye and felt a wave of anxiety wash over her. Something was wrong. He seemed worried. He never acted like this and although she hated him, she would never turn him away if he was in trouble.

"Stubbsy, you're acting affy strange, are you ok?" she said taking a seat on the settee.

"Eh aye, sound man, nae worries," Stubbsy said trying to gain some composure, but failing miserably. "Actually no, things aren't fine," he confessed, nervously rubbing his sweaty hands together.

"God Stubbs, what's the matter? Is it Stevie, is he ok?" Lisa asked frantically.

"No, Stevie's fine, its, ehm, well it's me, well me and you… it's… Look Lisa, ahm not great at this type of thing."

Lisa raised an eyebrow to show she didn't quite believe Stubbs's assertion that he couldn't talk to girls.

"Aye, awrite, when it's bullshit, am yer man, but when it's this? Lisa look, am so sorry for the way ah treated you that night you came home from your date. Ah was a prick, a complete prick and ah wish ah could take it back." Lisa looked at this big hulk humbling himself in front of her and felt elated inside.

"He tried to rape me, you know?" Lisa said quietly, reliving certain moments from that horrible night.

"Ah know he did hen, but believe me, he won't do it again."

Lisa looked at him for a second, confused as to what he meant, and then it dawned on her.

"You... it was you that..."

Stubbs put a finger to his lips to silence her.

"There's cops everywhere. You watch what you're saying," he said playfully. Lisa didn't know what to say. He had, not for the first time, put his neck on the line for her. Maybe she was wrong about him; maybe he wasn't the arsehole she thought he was after all.

"Listen," Stubbsy said, restoring himself to his normal confidence level, "let me take you out tonight, for a drink. Not in Motherwell, but in town, somewhere nice, just you and me, as mates, what do you think?"

Lisa pretended to weight up the options, but for the first time in ages she felt like going out, getting drunk, with STUBBSY! "That would be nice, just let me go get changed. There's beer in the fridge, and you can change that daft CD if you like."

Stubbsy glanced towards the stereo. It was playing some dark brooding music that he knew could only be of Stevie's liking.

Lisa came into living room after quickly freshening up. She was dressed to the level of 'drinks with mates', which was somewhere above normal college clothes, but just below big night out gear. Stubbsy didn't mind, he thought she looked stunning.

The recent heatwave Motherwell had enjoyed had made a comeback after a week of drizzly rain, and at half-past six Stubbsy and Lisa enjoyed a leisurely walk up Merry Street towards the train station. They didn't walk hand-in-hand, but to a casual passerby they exuded the closeness of two long-term lovers. They timed the train nicely as it rumbled into platform two. Just as they were about to board, Stubbsy stopped Lisa and lightly grabbed hold of her arm.

"Lisa, can ah ask you a favour?"

"Uh huh?"

"Can you call me Gary?"

"Of course ah can, Gary," Lisa laughed.

The two Motherwell souls boarded the 18:46 to Dalmuir for a night out in Glasgow. It would be the night that would change both their lives forever.

CHAPTER 13

SUNSHINE SICKNESS

ALISTAIR SEETHED SILENTLY AS AGNES'S monosyllabic tones trilled through him like a pneumatic road drill.

"That's wee Adele jist phoned there, Alastair. The perr wee sowel's no well, up aw nite wi' the cauld."

He stared at Agnes incredulously for a second, hoping to detect at least a hint of knowing sarcasm. None was forthcoming. It was as if she actually *believed* Adele's story, even though this was the third Friday in two months she had failed to turn up for her shift. This was the same Adele who thought nothing of skiving from her store duties to go brazenly into Alistair's office, use his computer to post updates on her Bebo page, where she would announce her hatred of both him and her job to her equally docile friends.

Adele wasn't the only one. The recent good weather had seen a thirty percent rise in absenteeism, the worst he had seen since he joined the company. They were six members of staff down today and he knew the warm weather would mean that the shop would be busier than normal. Such adverse circumstances usually brought the best out in Alistair, but today he just didn't seem have the energy to deal with it. He had pencilled in a Dairy stock check in the morning, had a disciplinary with Adam Bell, who had been accused of stealing four boxes of King-size Mayfairs from the kiosk at lunch time, and was supposed to be going for a meal with Marie at Dalziel Park tonight. He picked up the phone, took a deep breath and dialled his home number.

"Marie, hi, how are you?" he said nervously.

"I'm fine, Alistair, why are you phoning? You only ever phone with bad news. Now, don't even try to tell me you can't make it tonight, don't you dare!"

"We've had six call-offs, Marie, there's nothing I can do. I can't leave the place," Alistair said sheepishly.

"But you can leave me Alistair, sitting on my tod again on a Saturday night. I am sick of it Alistair," Marie groaned.

"I'll make it up to you, I promise," Alistair said eagerly as he heard his wife slam the phone down.

Marie looked heavenwards and let out a frustrated cry. Why was she being such a bitch? Alistair didn't deserve her constant whining, he was only doing his job. But she was scared. She was scared that with every passing day she felt her love for Alistair wane. The thought of living her life without him had once terrified her, not through fear of her own impending loneliness, but for Alistair, and how he would cope on his own without her. But now she felt as if she was fighting a losing battle. The end was in sight, and no amount of counselling, talks, or heart-to-hearts was going to change it.

Stevie looked at the *Daily Record* gig guide and cursed his luck. Trust him to be working on the night his favourite new band came to town. He had first heard Witness on Steve Lamaq's evening session and found himself being drawn to their singer Gerard Starkey's beautiful voice. He immediately went out and bought their debut album *Before the Calm*. It was a dark, soulful record that, on closer inspection, also contained some of the most insightful and clever lyrics he had ever heard. They were playing tonight in King Tut's Wah Wah Hut and he wouldn't be there. He was working a twelve-to-eight shift, which left him little to no time to make his way into town. He had hoped that there may have been an outside chance of getting away early if they were quiet enough. Some hope. Alistair had asked him to cover the back shop for him as he was busy with a disciplinary. This along with the fact that six people had phoned in sick meant that it would be a miracle if would get finished at eight, never mind any earlier.

He had been taking on more and more responsibilities in the store to help Alistair out. His approval into Strathclyde University and his continuing involvement with Jack's impact team meant that he was more relaxed about accepting Alistair's invite into taking a more senior role in the everyday mechanics of Morrisons Wishaw, confident that he had done enough outside the store to offset any chance of descending into the nightmare scenario of carving out a career in the retail industry. He liked Alistair, and felt the staff gave him a hard time that was both unjust and unfair. He had actually said as much at a night out he had endured with the staff a few weeks back. He gathered them round and told them, in no uncertain terms, what he thought of them and their treatment of Alistair and that he hoped their attitude towards him would improve. The female staff, young and old, collectively swooned as he addressed them, nodding their heads vigorously, so delighted they were that the hottest guy at work had finally attended a night out. The male contingent was less receptive. Who did this prick think he was? Coming to their night and dishing out the orders? The answer, they grudgingly conceded, was that he was Stubbsy's mate, from Leven Street, which meant he could say whatever the fuck he liked.

Alistair summoned Adam King into his office for the beginning of what he expected to be a swift disciplinary procedure. He was accused of stealing cigarettes from the kiosk. 'Accused' was giving Adam more credit than was due. The security cameras had caught him blatantly putting the four boxes into his hold-all.

"Ok, Adam, the reason you're here is that you have been accused of stealing contraband from the store. Now, before we go any further, do you wish to have your union representative present?" Alistair said professionally.

"Eh ahm no in the union, seven pound fifty a month? Fuck that."

Alastair winced at Adam's coarseness. He believed you could tell everything you needed to know about an employee by their attitude towards the trade union that represented them. As management, he was seen as the enemy of the union, but he honestly believed that they were vital in creating a solid workforce. Union input gave the management an insight into how the workers felt and what their needs were. Even though, Alistair conceded, their demands could not always be met, striking a balance was always a productive way to go forward.

"Look, Adam," Alistair said wearily, realising that the person before him was a lost cause. "I'll put in your language if it helps. You're fucked mate. The security cameras caught you taking the cigarettes, which is a criminal offence."

"Naw bit," Adam said frantically.

"Naw bit, nothing, Adam. Even if you hadn't stolen the fags, you were on your way out, pal. Your sickness record, time keeping and general performance have been appalling. Now you will be suspended for a month without pay, until Human Resources figure out what to do with you. My advice, Adam, is you quit while you're ahead, hand in your notice and go quietly."

"Aye," Adam said through gritted teeth, all the time thinking, "You fuckin die for this, you cunt."

Stevie managed to get out the store at quarter past eight, leaving Alistair and the night shift to clear up the mess from the day's mayhem. He strolled down towards Wishaw Main Street. The sun was still shining, but the heat had died down to a more comfortable level. He knew he had missed his chance of getting into Glasgow for the gig, but fancied a pint. Wishaw was hardly a hotbed for Saturday night entertainment, but it did at least have a better choice than Motherwell. He weighed up his options, knowing full well that Girdwood's was the only one that was realistically viable. Just as he was about to turn into Hill Street, he heard a car horn beep and a white Clio, one he recognised, pulled up beside him. It was Marie, Alistair's wife.

"Hi Stevie, do you need a lift, I'm heading down Motherwell way?" she called from behind her Gucci shades.

Stevie weighed up his options. A five-minute car journey with his boss's stunning wife or a couple of stale pints of Diesel with the Gothic grease-bags that had made Girdwood's their own.

"Eh aye, that would great, if it's not too much trouble," he said, trying not to stare at Marie's long tanned legs. She was wearing a short denim skirt and brown, heeled sandals and looked amazing. How on earth did Alistair end up with her?

"Heading out tonight?" Marie asked as she guided her car down Glasgow Road.

"Well, ah was supposed to go see a band in town, but ahm too late now," Stevie said.

"Yeah, which band?" Marie asked.

"Och, a band called Witness, you wouldn't have heard of them," Stevie said, worrying that he may sound slightly pretentious.

"Oh aye, they supported The Verve in the Barras did they not?" Marie replied.

"You saw them? Live?" Stevie said incredulously. He couldn't believe it. Someone other than himself knew who Witness was, and it was Alistair's wife!

"Well," Marie said, as she began to recount the story, "you know the Delgaldos?"

"Aye, ah love them," Stevie said.

"Well, the girl who plays flute with them teaches the kids at the school I work in once a week. She copied a bunch of CDs for me, one of which was The Verve. I got really into it and Alistair and I went to see them. That band you just said were supporting, and they were all right from what I can remember."

Stevie thought about this for a second. Alistair – the wettest, most straight-laced geek he had ever met – had a steady job, a brand new car, a gorgeous wife and had seen Witness live. The world wasn't fair.

"So what about you, any plans for tonight?" Stevie asked casually.

"Pfffft, I was supposed to be going for a romantic meal with my husband but he has, shall we say, other things on his mind." They both looked at each other for a second, then simultaneously burst out laughing.

"Oh that man." Marie sighed. "I don't know what I'm going to do with him. That's where I was just now, dropping some dinner off for him. He'll end up staying there all night," she said, like a mother talking about her son who doesn't want to come home from the swing park.

"He's a good guy, he works hard," Stevie said.

"Mmmm, too hard methinks," Marie said almost to herself. "Oh fuck this, fancy going for a drink somewhere?" she not so much asked, as demanded.

"Eh aye, where do you want to go?" Stevie asked, slightly startled.

"Where I was supposed to be going, Dalziel Park. It's quiet there. Can't have people talking now Steven, can we?" she teased.

Stevie laughed off the flirtatious manner of Marie's question, whilst consciously rubbing his right pocket. He had about twenty-eight pounds on him, which should be enough for at least two drinks in that establishment.

Once they had parked the car they made their way up towards the bar area. Two golfers who had finished their round nudged and winked at one another as they watched Marie's swaggering saunter that, though it seemed so natural, could have easily came straight from a Milan catwalk. She was a goddess and Stevie couldn't quite believe what he was doing. Going for an innocent drink with your boss's beautiful wife? He knew it was wrong but something seemed to keep any negative thoughts he had at bay.

"Are we going to regret this, Marie?" Stevie asked as he placed a small glass of white Chardonnay on the table

"Hopefully." Marie laughed as she drowned her drink in one go.

CHAPTER 14

STUBBS AND LISA: A MOTHERWELL LOVE STORY (PART TWO)

THE SUN SPLASHED THROUGH THE OFFICES and old style tenement buildings at the west side of St Vincent Street, making it feel like a summer's night in a place that wasn't Glasgow. It was Friday night and those of a more spiritual nature would be most likely to conclude that tonight, something, just something, was in the air.

Barry slid onto the chair behind the bar in Remo's, put his head in his hands and felt the cold sweat slowly emit from his aching pores as the noise from the corner slowly started to get louder and louder. He had been out with Brian last night. Since moving through to Glasgow to get ready for university he had been out nearly every night. He felt so much more liberated and free. Telling his parents about his sexuality was difficult, but at least he could stop being someone he wasn't and start to live his life his way. There was, he reflected, no better place to do it than in Glasgow. The gay scene here was vibrant and fresh and didn't have the snooty pretentiousness he had encountered on trips to Brighton and London. He had cruised a few guys since moving here, but none could compare to Brian.

They'd hooked up at the Optimo a few weeks past and had been inseparable ever since. They had gone out last night and overdone it with the shots. Now he was struggling. He thought that because his shift didn't start till seven and he only had to work till ten, he would breeze through it. This was also the weekend of the All Tomorrow's Parties festival, which meant most of their usual clientele would be at the festival now or in Nice and Sleazies getting ready to head up later.

What he didn't account for was the couple who had come in just as his shift began. At first he thought they were run-of-the-mill Weedgies, but on closer inspection he could hear a slight drawl in their accent which he couldn't quite place. He was also unfamiliar with some of the phrases they used. Everything seemed to be "miles out" and the guy with the blond hair had this annoying habit of ending most of his sentences with something that sounded like "masuuun". What the fuck language was this? Barry thought the girl looked quite nice and was really friendly when she came to the bar. The guy on the other hand was a complete wanker. When he was passing to go to the toilet, he looked at Barry's brand new Calvin Klein boxer shorts that were tastefully fitted over his hanging Firetrap denims.

"Haw, sir," he hissed. "Pull yer jeans up, fir fuck sake," the cretin ordered.

Barry waited till he had passed and half-heartedly gave him the finger. Three more hours of this shite and he would be home in his flat on Queen Margaret Drive, snuggled up with Brian, smoking some quality weed and forgetting all about the scumbags he had to deal with on a part-time basis.

"OK, what ah don't get is handbags," Stubbsy said, hoping to extract some kind of reaction from Lisa. She didn't disappoint.

"What do you mean you don't 'get' them. Of course you don't. Why would any man want to go out and get a handbag?" Lisa said, hoping he would take the bait.

"Eh naw, what ah mean is ah don't *get* them," Stubbsy said, slightly confused.

"Ha ha, yeah ah know what you mean. Ok Stub... sorry, Gary, tell me exactly what you don't get about ladies' handbags."

"Well, ah don't understand why lassies get so excited and spend daft amounts of money buying them. They don't bring anything to the table. Ah mean, take it from me, there hasn't been one guy in history who has clocked a wee bird and thought 'Fuckin hell, look at the handbag on that!'"

"Ah that's the thing though Stub... sorry, Gary," Lisa said, trying to stifle a laugh at the clumsy one-sidedness of Stubbsy's argument. "We don't spend money on handbags to impress the boys; we do it to be the envy of the girls. You see, if you're on a night out and you have a cute little Gucci or Prada handbag you're basically saying to all the other females in the place 'Yes, I know you love my handbag, I know you want my handbag, but you can't have it because it's mine, mwaaha'!"

Stubbsy shook his head and raised his hands in defeat. He was a having a good night. They'd only had about three or four drinks so far, but already he was feeling giddy. If this was any other girl he would have been giving her every line in the book. But not with Lisa. He was happy to bide his time. He didn't want to blow it and to come on too strong. He played a blinder on the train journey in. He was calm and respectful and told her that he realised they were just friends and how happy he was that he could genuinely call her that. And the thing was, he meant it. He wanted her, obviously, but just being here with her was enough. When he was with her the whole world was a better place and his attitude to everyone and everything was different. Even the wee poofy guy behind the bar couldn't spoil his night.

Stubbsy wasn't one of these weird, homophobic guys who felt that a man's masculinity was best measured by his hatred and disdain for homosexuals. Yet, despite this, he had no time whatsoever for these touchy-feely, fag-hag types who simply must have a gay friend and took great pleasure in announcing the fact that they have a "gay pal". "He's your pal or he's not your pal, what the fuck's the gay bit got to do with it?" Stubbsy thought .

The wee guy behind the bar would normally have done Stubbsy's head in, all surly and aloof. But tonight he couldn't care less and even tried to help the guy, telling him that his jeans had fallen down. Why didn't he wear a belt?

Lisa went to the toilet to touch up her make-up. This had to be one of the most surreal days of her life. She woke up this morning with nothing but hatred towards Stubbsy, but now she was in a pub in Glasgow with him, calling him Gary and melting inside every time she caught a glimpse of his ocean blue eyes. The only fly in the ointment was on the train in when he said he was happy to "just be friends". She'd agreed with him, of course, well, she had to. But deep down she was thinking, "No, I don't want to be your friend anymore. I want *you*. I want to touch and play with you. I want to feel you inside me, and naked laying next me."

"Right, Gary boy," Lisa said returning to her seat with a pint of cold Guinness and a glass of rosy with ice. "Tell me something about yourself that you haven't told anyone before."

Stubbsy thought about this for a minute. In normal circumstances, when faced with a question which demanded an honest answer, he would instinctively make something up. With Lisa, it was different. He couldn't be anything other than honest with her.

"Ah get scared sometimes," Stubbsy said plainly.

"Scared?" Lisa laughed dismissively. "What in God's name scares you?" The very notion of Stubbsy being scared of anything seemed too ridiculous for words.

"Och, just people and that, Stevie mainly," Stubbsy confessed, taking a healthy gulp of Guinness.

This was weird; Lisa had never seen Stubbsy like this before. So solemn, so exposed. "Gary, why on earth would you be scared of Stevie, that's just daft," Lisa said seriously.

"Ahm not scared of him as a person. But ahm shit scared of losing him. Ah mean, the books, the music, the films he's into, ah just don't get it. And the politics? He blabbers on for ages about it sometimes and ahm sitting there, totally clueless. Ah noticed him coming out of his shell lately and ahm worried he'll think 'why am ah hanging about with this deadbeat?' Ah don't think ah could handle that."

Lisa stared at Stubbsy for a second then took him by the hand. "Now you look here, Gary Stubbs. You are the best friend Stevie has ever had. The things you have done for him over the years goes way beyond friendship. And besides, Stevie's not the type of person who would drop his best friend just like that." Lisa suddenly realised she had been holding his hand for over a minute and coolly tried to let go.

"Eh you want to move on somewhere else?" Stubbsy said, trying to break the awkwardness of intimacy.

"Yeah, cool, ahm going to nip to the loo."

Lisa went for a pee and, after washing her hands, she checked herself in the mirror once more. As she tried to decide whether the spot on her lip had grown bigger, a flyer on the door caught her eye.

KING TUTS WAH WAH HUT

FRIDAY 27TH MAY

WITNESS + THE CHAMELEONS

LISA COULDN'T BELIEVE IT: THE BAND Stevie hadn't stopped listening to and banging on about were playing just up the road. How funny would it be if Stubbsy and she went to see them? Stevie would be gutted!

"Right, you, c'mon, we're going to the King Tut's Wah Wah Hut," she said to Stubbsy, slipping her cardigan on and pointing to the door.

When Lisa explained why they were going there, Stubbsy was delighted. He phoned up Stevie to wind him up. It went straight to voicemail, so putting on his best West End Glasgow University accent, the one where every sentence is a question, he left him a message.

"Eh hi Steve, it's your friend Gary here? Yeah, Lisa and ah were, like, thinking, like, it would be, like, cool? If we like went to see a band or something? In, like, King Tut's or something? Do you, like, know if, like, there's any bands like playing there tonight or something?"

Lisa was in stitches. She used to resent Stubbsy's humour, resent the fact that she couldn't enjoy it the way others did, but now she was milking it for what it was worth. On the way up St Vincent Street, they passed a young guy with a "homeless and hungry" sign at his knees. Stubbsy dragged Lisa to a Subway across the road. When he gave the homeless man the sandwich he'd bought, he wrapped a ten pound note around it.

"Right, ya wee cunt, ye can scrub out the hungry bit now, nae false advertising," he said as Lisa shook her head in bewilderment. Like him or not, Stubbsy was a one-off.

When they finally found the venue, after walking past it three times, they paid their money at the door and headed downstairs to where the band were about to come on. Lisa was surprised to see that it was pretty empty, yet disappointed there weren't any seats left. The only thing Lisa could say about the support band, who were giving it their all on the stage, was that they sounded like the type of band Stevie would like. She knew Stubbsy agreed when she saw him tie and pull an imaginary noose round his neck. The support band finished their set and were replaced by some hippy types who banged on drums, stepped on pedals and pulled on wires. Lisa found them quite annoying, but assumed they knew what they were doing.

Eventually, Witness shuffled on to the stage, with singer Gerry Starkey offering a meek "All right?" Those who were sitting down slowly began to make their way onto the floor. Stubbs was about to guide Lisa to one of the available chairs, when the band started on ear-blistering version of 'Scars'. Suddenly the crowd came to life. Cheers of "Get in!" and "Come on!" were coming from all corners of the venue. Lisa and Stubbs looked at each other and immediately felt the electricity in the air. For her part, Lisa was amazed that this music, which had sounded so morbid when listened to on CD, could feel so thrilling when played live. Stubbsy was, despite himself, zoning into the lyrics that he could barely make out. It was as if he was singing to him personally, about his love for Motherwell and how local life was more important than anything else in the world.

The songs kept coming, each one more awe-inspiring than the last. What started as a joke to wind up Stevie, was fast becoming the most amazing experience they had ever encountered. Stubbsy broke off to go get some drinks. When he arrived back, singer Gerry Starkey, who had remained silent throughout the gig, announced the next song as 'So Far Gone'. The lights went down low and the crowd roared their approval. The song started slowly at first, then began to build momentum. A solitary blue light shone on the lead singer. Stubbsy was transfixed by the silhouette effect it had on Lisa. It made her even more beautiful. They were both sweating profusely, but Stubbs couldn't hold back any longer. He slowly slid his hands under her blouse and on to her waist, gently pulling her close to him and kissing her on the neck.

Lisa responded by tilting her head back towards him and closing her eyes in ecstasy at the feel of Stubbsy's lips on her skin. They twisted naturally towards each other and embraced in a long passionate kiss as the music kicked into a higher gear and the lights began to shine all around them. When they finally separated they self-consciously looked to see if anyone had noticed their obvious first flush of intimacy, only to find other couples in similar embraces. The band finished the song and left the stage. Lisa and Stubbsy, who were unfamiliar with the rock gig setup, assumed that this was the end of the show and left the venue hand-in-hand, oblivious to the fact that Witness were still to come on for an encore.

Once outside, the evening air had turned cooler and Lisa cuddled as closely into Stubbsy as she could to try and stay warm. They walked together in silence up to the nearest taxi rank. So engrossed in each other they were that they failed to acknowledge the beggar that Stubbsy had been so generous to before, lying flat out on the pavement, eyes a-glaze and the Subway sandwich still in its wrapper. In the taxi on the way home, Lisa dozed in and out of a drunken sleep, all the time perching her head comfortably on Stubbsy's shoulder.

When they arrived in Motherwell, Stubbsy directed the taxi driver to Merry Street to where Stevie and Lisa's flat was. He had already paid the driver up front, but asked him to wait outside while he saw Lisa to her door.

"Why don't you come in, ah don't want you to go," Lisa pleaded.

"Ah can't. I am working tomorrow and I've got the van. Listen, ah knock off at twelve. Why don't ah come round here. We can go for lunch up the Tav, invite Mr Costello along and tell him what an amazing gig he missed," Stubbsy said, pulling Lisa towards him. "Ah love you, Lisa."

Lisa took Stubbsy's face in her hands and kissed him deeply. "See you tomorrow, Gary," she said, kissing him gently on the head one last time.

When he got back on the street the taxi had disappeared. This would have usually enraged Stubbsy, but tonight he couldn't care less. He would take the relatively short walk to Leven Street and enjoy every minute of it.

Lisa lay in her bed and tried to calm her beating heart. She had never felt so natural and happy. Plans were going through her head. Holidays, houses, marriage and families. She didn't know if she would sleep tonight, but if she did, her dreams would be filled with only one man. Gary. Her Gary.

Greenacres had seen its status as Motherwell's most sought after place to live diminish over the years, as the Barrett four- and five-bedroom house estates that had sprung up everywhere in the town attracted the younger generation of house buyers. These wide-eyed, newlyweds had not so much money to burn, but banks and building societies that were willing to give them credit to burn, which some of the newlyweds, unfortunately, thought was the same thing. Jean and Albert had seen them all come and go over the years. Some good friends and neighbours had passed on only to be replaced by younger, less desirable or, even worse, foreign individuals. The one tradition that they had managed to keep intact was their annual summer barbeque. Tonight's gathering was, all things considered, a success. In fact, if it hadn't been for Old Joe's behaviour, the night would have been an unqualified triumph.

Mary had read somewhere that the divorce rate in Great Britain was now at an all-time high with almost 22% of British marriages ending in divorce. After her husband Joe's latest embarrassing episode, she thought that adding to that sad statistic maybe wouldn't be such a bad idea. They had been invited to Jean and Albert's barbeque, as they were every year. It started well enough. Joe had promised not to drink and took the car as a token of his intentions. Everything was fine until Jean's granddaughter and friends arrived. Joe, who had the habit of thinking he was still a teenager himself, started knocking back the whiskey and tried to grab one of the poor girls up for a dance. She rightly slapped him across the dish. The night was over after that.

On the way home Mary had to drive as Joe was completely hammered. As they drove up Orchard Street he leaned over towards Jean and tried the grab the steering wheel. Mary managed to wrestle him off.

"Pull over woman, ah need to go," Joe slobbered to his wife.

"Joe please, ahm trying to drive, you'll have to wait," she said impatiently.

"PULLLLOVVERR!" Joe roared as he lunged towards the steering well. Mary lost control of the car as it sped head first towards The Duchess Park. She heard an almighty thump, as if they had hit something big. An animal or a lamppost? Mary struggled from the car and went to inspect. To her horror she realised it wasn't either. She pulled out her mobile phone and dialled 999.

The ambulance that was dispatched from the Muirhouse depot was there in a matter of minutes. They did everything they could to save the individual but it was too late. In Wishaw General Accident and Emergency department, Gary John Stubbs was pronounced dead at 00:05 Saturday morning.

CHAPTER 15

STEVIE COSTELLO'S TEAR OF THE YEAR

ALISTAIR RUBBED THE SWEAT AWAY from his brow and breathed a heavy breath. He was tired from what had proved to be one of the most difficult days of his working life. He ignored Colin and Graeme who were saying sarcastic good-byes to him from the bakery aisle. He'd had to stay on an extra two hours to try and bring some kind of order to the store, much to the disgruntlement of the nightshift. He made his way towards his car, flicked his phone on and proceeded to phone his wife Marie. As his finger hovered above her number he flicked the phone down. "Fuck it," he thought, "fuck her and fuck them, fuck the lot of them."

For the first time in his life, Alistair was tired. Tired of his work, tired of his wife, tired of his whole existence. He was beginning to think his every effort to make the world a better place was being slammed back into his face. He was sick of it and knew that something had to change. As he fiddled with his keys he heard someone shuffle behind him. Before he had a chance to properly turn and see who it was he felt a hand come towards him and clasp his jaw. The grip was so hard that Alistair struggled to breath. In shock, he managed to make out his assailant.

"Ahm fucked? Ahm fucked? Who's fucked noo ya cunt?" Adam said as he crashed his head into the bridge of Alistair's nose, breaking it instantly. Alistair fell back to the ground, his eyes blurred and his senses in disarray. Adam and his friends had waited outside the Morrisons car park for Alistair, biding their time, waiting for the opportunity to exact revenge for Adam's dismissal.

"Fuckin chucked oot the hoose cause ay you, ya cunt" Adam said aiming a swift, but deadly kick to Alistair midriff. He reeled over in agony and tried to gain some control, but the pain was too intense and all he could do was cry.

"P... p... p... please, please stop... am... I... please..." Through the excruciating pain, Alistair began having flashbacks to his school days. This wasn't the first time he had been on the end of a physical beating from the likes of Adam King. Every night he had to run the frightening gauntlet as the head boys from his year cruelly singled him out for their relentless bullying. Some nights he was lucky and made it home safe. When they did manage to catch him, they would dish out beatings of varying degrees of violence. The physical pain of these beating were bad enough, but they paled into insignificance when compared to the pain of seeing the anguish on his father's face as he realised his son was living his life in fear. That his son was already one of life's victims. Now, Alistair thought, Marie would be the one who looked on him with helpless pity. The thought crushed him.

"Whit's yer favourite team in the Premiership then, ya cunt?" Adam sneered.

"W... what?" Alistair stammered.

"FAVOURITE TEAM IN THE PREMIERSHIP, YA DAFT CUNT?" Adam screamed into Alistair's face, flecks of spit flying into the night.

"What... I don't, what?"

"Say Chelsea, ya cunt," Adam said slowly.

"I... what?" Alistair groaned, totally confused as to what Adam wanted from him.

"SAYFUCKINCHELSEAYACUNT!" Adam shouted ferociously.

"Ch... Ch... Chelsea," Alistair groaned.

"Ha, ah'll gie ye fuckin Chelsea, ya cunt," Adam said whilst pulling out a gleaming blade from his pocket. In one swift move he slit each of Alistair's cheeks.

Alistair screamed in pain and tried in vain to hold his face together as blood and loose skin escaped between his fingers. His howls had attracted some Saturday night passers-by who ran to his aid. Adam and his friends saw the amount of blood that was pouring from Alistair's face and made a run for it. A woman who had come to help Alistair cradled his head on her lap while her boyfriend phoned an ambulance. Saturday nights were usually very busy at Wishaw General Hospital; tonight would be no different.

Stevie and Marie sat in the Dalziel Park, quietly enjoying the solitude such a place of respectability can bring. They had been here for over an hour now and both were pleasantly surprised at how at ease they were in each other's company. After milling over the state of her marriage with Alistair, Marie felt that she had been talking about herself far too long. With this in mind she switched the conversation away from herself and on to Stevie.

"So, the girl who killed herself, the politician's daughter, was she your girlfriend?" she asked casually.

"She was once yeah, but not when she done what she did, we split about two weeks before it," Stevie said, gulping the last of his pint of lager.

"And do you think that was why she did it?" Marie asked carefully.

"No, she actually split up with me. She had no hang-ups about it, and gave me no reason to believe she would take her own life."

"So why then, why do you think she did it?" Marie said, suddenly intrigued.

"Absolutely no idea, ah've gone over it time and time again, but it's still a fuckin mystery. Ah've actually resigned myself to the fact that ah'll never know."

Marie gave Stevie a sympathetic half smile, and squeezed his hand. Stevie took another sip of his pint and began telling Marie everything. He told her about his mum and how she left him at such a young age; about the fractured nature of his relationship with his father. He spoke about Stubbsy and Lisa, about how much both their friendships meant to him and his hope that they both would one day get along. He then spoke about the thing that had been laying so heavily on his mind for so long.

"Ah didn't cry. At Clare's funeral, ah didn't shed one tear. Ah wanted to, definitely felt like it, but ah just couldn't, man."

Marie looked at this stranger beside her and felt as if she had known him all her life.

"Some would see that as quite noble Stevie, don't beat yourself up over it," Marie said softly.

"Ahm not a heartless person, Marie, and don't want anyone thinking ah am," Stevie said lowering his head. Marie moved closer to him and lifted his chin with her finger and thumb.

"You're not heartless, Stevie, don't let me hear you say that again". They both looked at each other for what seemed like a lifetime, wondering what the night was going to bring next. Just then Marie's phone began to vibrate. It was Alistair's work number.

"It's Alistair, my God he's still at work... Hello... wha... WHAT? No, no, ok, ok, I'll go straight away."

"What's wrong? What's happened?" Stevie said anxiously as he watched the colour drain from Marie's face.

"It's Alistair, he's been jumped outside the store, they took him to Accident and Emergency in the Wishaw General. I'll have to go," Marie said worriedly.

"Ok, ah'll come with you," Stevie said grabbing his jacket.

When they arrived at the hospital it was bursting at the seams. Marie hurried to the front desk and gave her details to the nurse. She asked them both to take a seat. After about an hour of waiting a young Asian doctor came towards the sitting area.

"Mrs Blaney?" he called towards them.

"Yes, yes, how is he? How is my husband?" Marie asked frantically.

"Mrs Blaney, please take a seat," the doctor said politely. "My name is Doctor Arhiem. Your husband was brought to us earlier this evening after being on the receiving end of a severe beating. He has suffered two broken ribs, swelling to the right testicle and significant lacerations to both cheeks. Mrs Blaney, your husband has lost a lot of blood. He has been cut open on each side of his face with a sharp object and I am afraid the likelihood is it will leave visible scars. He is conscious, but finding it very difficult to communicate. The police have been in to question him. You may go in and see him now," he said turning and heading busily down another corridor.

Marie dropped back onto her seat and began to sob.

"Why? Why Alistair?" she thought. "Why couldn't people leave him alone, or appreciate him for what he was. He was a good man and all he wanted to do was help others. Why couldn't people see that?"

She walked into the ward where he was being treated. At first she couldn't find his bed. It wasn't till she saw his name above one of the beds did she know. Alistair was unrecognisable. Both his eyes were swollen and he had two black stitched scars trained across his face.

"Alistair," Marie whispered, grabbing lightly for his hand. "It's Marie, what happened? What have they done, Alistair?"

After a lulled silence, only broken by his laboured breathing, Alistair, through his pain and bruising, slowly began to speak.

"Marie," he said quietly, "it's over."

Then he turned his face away, leaving Marie sad and broken. She let go of his hand and sat staring at the man lying in his bed, the man who was about to become her ex-husband. She silently moved towards the exit of the ward. She turned to her husband in his perilous state. It would be the last time she ever laid eyes on him.

Del Johnson took the obs of the last elderly patient in the female respiratory ward and carefully entered the results into the patient's cardex. It had been a hard shift, a horrible shift in fact. He couldn't believe that, at the start of his last week of placement, his old witch of a mentor had put him on the Friday night shift. Despite trying not to think about what Tommy and the rest of the boys would be up to now, he couldn't help it. They were heading down to the Mad Shaker night they had accidentally stumbled on last month when they were having a few quite pints in the Electric Bar. It was run by the Fenians with Oasis haircuts who, although Del thought were all right, had an undignified amount of ginger hair in their midst. What had caught Del, Tommy and rest of the boys' attention was the ice cool indie chicks bopping on the dance floor to the old sixties tunes. How he wished he was amongst them tonight.

Any self-pitying Del put on himself evaporated about ten o'clock when he went down to the front door for a cigarette. While minding his own business he was approached by Jim Clark, a porter from Corsington

Gardens he had known off and on for a few years now. His face was ashen and he was running his hands through his hair desperately.

"Heard the news?" he said dolefully.

"No, whit's the matter, Jim, what's happened?" Del said.

"Fuckin big Stubbsy, by the way, car crash, passed away in the ambulance," Jim said sadly.

Del waited a second just to make sure he had heard Jim properly.

"Whit, Stubbsy fae Leven Street? Big Stubbsy? Yir joking me, man, tell me yer joking, Jim?" Del said trying to take the news in.

"No jokin', by the way, fuckin tragic, man."

Del went back up to the ward hardly able to take the news in. He knew big Stubbsy well, used to play fives with him a few years back. He was one of the funniest guys he had ever known. The talk was that he was a hard bastard to go with it. However, Del never saw that side. All he could remember was the big honest tryer on the five-a-side pitch who would take the piss from start to finish and always made sure everyone had a lift home. His mind for the rest of the shift was filled with the tragic loss of someone so young and how it put things into perspective.

At about twelve-thirty he left the ward to go get a cold drink. As he approached the vending machine, he saw an old face from school. Realising who it was, Del felt an unattainable sadness wash over him.

Stevie had left Marie with Alistair, figuring there was nothing he could do and that now wasn't the best time for Alistair to find out that, whilst he was slogging his guts out in the supermarket, his newly appointed Produce Assistant Team Leader had spent a cosy, yet mainly innocent, night with his wife. Poor Alistair, he thought, what scumbag would do such a thing. Typical Wishaw, typical Motherwell.

Before he left the hospital, he stopped at a vending machine to buy himself a Diet Coke. The alcohol from the pints he had drunk earlier was beginning to run low, leaving him with a killer thirst. As he fiddled into his pocket for some change, he could feel someone walk towards him slowly. It was only till the person was in earshot did he turn round to see who it was. He recognised him immediately. Big Del Johnson was a year above him at school. The last time they spoke was at the last Floorshaker. Stevie always had him down as a bit of a sport Billy and was surprised to see him at such a leftfield club night.

"Del, how's tricks mate?" Stevie asked brightly.

Del looked at him strangely and lightly held Stevie by the arm.

"Eh ahm fine mate, how are you Stevie, how are you?" Del said solemnly. Stevie looked at Del's hand on his arm and the look of dejected pity on his face. Something wasn't right.

"Am fine, Del, whit's wrong mate? You look shattered, son," Stevie said.

"Stubbsy, ahm so sorry, man," Del said shaking his head. Stevie's eyes widened and felt his stomach fall through his shoes.

"Del, what do you mean 'Stubbsy'? Whit's happened?" Stevie said anxiously.

Del stared at Stevie for moment. He didn't know. He didn't know about the accident. Del had been given a talk at Uni about handling bereavement at the front line. What this meant was, as a nurse, you will find yourself in situations where you are the first contact a person may have after being told of a loved one's death. He didn't think he would have to use it at such an early stage of his nursing career.

"Oh Stevie man, there's been an accident. Stubbs's been run over down Motherwell somewhere. Stevie, ahm sorry. Stubbsy died earlier."

Stevie began feel the walls spinning round him. He thought he was going to pass out. Pushing Del to one side, he began to run down the corridor looking for an exit. As he emerged out of the main entrance, black sheets of rain came hailing down on him. He thought he was going to be sick and eventually stumbled onto a nearby lamppost. He held onto it for dear life.

"NAAAAAAAAAAAAAAAAW, FUCKIN NAWW, STUBBSY MAN NAW, PLEASE NAW!" he yelled as he tried to scream the debilitating pain from his soul. He tried to push out the tears, tears that had eluded him for so long and would have given him the emotional release he so badly needed. But to his anger and frustration he couldn't cry. He just fell to knees, held his head in his hands and stared at the ground below.

At this point, Del had come running out the hospital along with an on-duty nurse. Trying to shield himself from the rain, he picked Stevie up, cradled him into his sizeable bulk and held him tenderly in his arms.

"S'awrite Stevie mate, ahm here, it's ok, son," he said as he manoeuvred Stevie back into the hospital.

Once they were inside, the nurse gently dried Stevie down with a hand towel. When she was satisfied that he was suitably dried, she began to softly make some inquiries.

"Steven, my name is Angela. I'm the nurse in charge of the ward your friend had been admitted to. Now, I know this is a hard time for you, but we need someone to come and get you. You're in no fit state to go home on your own. Your friend's family have been notified and are on their way. Is there anyone you would like us to phone?"

Stevie looked blankly at the nurse. Since his parents weren't around his emergency contact had always been his Aunt May and Uncle John, but he hadn't spoken to them in months and didn't want to bother them. He thought about Jack, and how he would know exactly what to do at times like this. Again, though, it didn't feel right. There was only one person he wanted to be with right now, even though it terrified him.

'Lisa, ah need speak to Lisa.'

CHAPTER 16

I NEVER KNEW YOU, YOU NEVER KNEW ME

THE RAIN THAT HAD STEADILY ENVELOPED WISHAW and Motherwell showed no sign of abating. Even though it wasn't a harsh rain, the people round these parts had experienced far worse; it could be best characterised by its relentlessness. Anyone who took one look at the sky could tell you that it was here to stay for a while yet. It provided a suitable backdrop for the mood that had descended on both towns. Not long after the bizarre suicide of the local MSP Jack Murray's daughter, Clare, they now found themselves engulfed with the grief of another young person's senseless death. Gary Stubbs was a popular young electrician from Leven Street, whose body was found outside The Duchess Park. He was twenty-three years old. Police were sure he had been the victim of a hit and run and the coronary report that outlined the nature of his injuries backed this theory up. They were still nowhere near finding who was driving the car. The only lead they had was a 999 call made from a pay-as-you-go mobile, which they now believed had been discarded.

Wild rumours had been circulating the towns as to who was driving the car and if it had been an accident. One line of inquiry the police followed up was a bouncer who had an altercation with Stubbs at the Motherwell Beer Festival a few months previously. When they questioned him, though, he had a cast-iron alibi: hundreds of revellers from Hamilton Palace, where he had been working that evening, had seen him. Another, more sinister line of inquiry, was the suggestion that the driver of the car was a young man from Muirhouse who had been left for dead in a freak attack in Wishaw Sports Centre. However, when the police went to his mother's house to question him he answered the door in a wheelchair and started wailing dementedly, "No, get him away, get him away!" when the police mentioned Stubbs' name. They were left to conclude that this had been an accident and that the driver of the car would be flushed out sooner rather than later.

Lisa pulled her legs under her stretched white T-shirt and pushed her lank, greasy hair away from her eyes. The steady beat of rain against the window of her old bedroom in her mum's house was the only noise she could hear except for the slow rumble that was emanating from her stomach. She couldn't remember the last time she had eaten anything. The only nourishment she had enjoyed over the last two days was the odd glass of water her mother had forced her to drink.

She was staring out towards the bus stop where wee Milky Tolan was once again huddling himself against the rain. He was tetchy and agitated. He always was when he left the house, thought Lisa. He wasn't when he returned. Lisa, like the rest of the people who were brought up in this scheme, knew the reason for this. Milky was a very open and very occasional heroin user. He never let it affect his personality or appearance and, to the casual outsider, he seemed like any other young working-class man. In fact, instead of being the boy old ladies would cross the street to avoid, Milky would often be seen helping those of a more senior vintage home with their shopping and checking they were safe in the cold winter months. Lisa remembered when he used to come over and help Dad with his garden. She loved how he wouldn't even ask if he needed a hand, he'd just pull his sleeves up and start mucking in. Lisa's dad wouldn't even look up, so used was he to Milky's welcomed efforts, although he would sometimes comment on how he thought that the laddie Malcolm was maybe "sniffin' that glue".

Lisa looked out at the garden. It looked limp and unkempt. What she wouldn't give to be able to go back to those innocent days, when the only thing she had to worry about was not being stung by the bees that were attracted to the beautiful flowers that made her dad's garden feel so wondrous and free.

Milky could help her. Help her end the pain, take away the sadness, the sadness of never knowing the one person she loved more than ever. For it was this that was killing her more than anything else. Not the pointless death or what she had lost. It was the fact that she never got the chance to know what she had lost. To be his girlfriend, his wife, the mother of his children, their children. Not knowing your soulmate? How could it be, Lord God, how could you make this happen, she thought. How could you take my beautiful boy from me before I had a chance to have him as mine?

"Hail Mary full of grace the Lord is with thee.

Blessed art thou amongst women

And blessed is the fruit of thy womb Jesus."

Lisa's mum, Patricia, held her Rosary beads close to her heart, closed her eyes and concentrated all her faith towards a resolution of her circumstances, towards the hope that her daughter would recover from the recent devastating events.

"Holy Mary, mother of God,

Pray for us sinners now,

And at the hour of our death, Amen."

Patricia had been praying the same prayer rhythmically. Her only movement was rubbing her thumb and finger around her holy beads. Anyone not familiar with Western Christian culture would think that this ritual was some kind of tribal chant, such was the hypnotic nature of its mantra. Patricia was worried sick about her daughter. Their relationship had been strained of late, ever since Lisa had found that her sister was actually her mother and Patricia was technically her grandmother. This all changed a few days back when Patricia had received a phone call from Lisa's flat mate, Stevie. He told her the horrifying news about their friend Stubbsy, who had been found dead at the weekend. Her heart had immediately gone out to Stevie. She had grown fond of him ever since Lisa and he had become friends, but also had her own private reason for keeping an eye on the poor boy who already had to deal with his girlfriend's suicide. What Patricia hadn't anticipated was the debilitating effect the death of this young man would have had on her daughter. Lisa had never conveyed any feeling for this person other than genuine contempt. But according to Stevie, when he broke the news to her, she almost collapsed to the point where Stevie thought he would have to phone an ambulance.

Since then, Patricia had taken Lisa home and all she had done was stare out of the window and, when she thought Patricia was out of earshot, sob uncontrollably into her pillow. It was a mystery, but Patricia reckoned that her daughter and this boy were closer than they made out. All she could do now was be there for her and hope she pulled through, but at the moment such a prospect seemed a long way off. Before making dinner, Patricia nervously thumbed the piece of paper in her hand that contained the phone number that she had never dialled. The number of a man she had never met, but had, none the less, made a solemn promise to. She approached the phone and nervously began to dial.

Tony looked over the sprawling vastness of his new winery from the comfort of his plush, newly refurbished offices and indulged himself in an uncharacteristic moment of self-satisfaction. He had relocated here six years ago after selling his advertising company that, despite being situated in the rather unfashionable surroundings of Newton Mairn's High Street, could count some of London's biggest fashion companies and high street names as clients. The relatively small piece of land he had bought on the famous Swan Valley Winery, which was nestled in the scenic area of Perth, Australia, was modest in comparison to what he was used to. The wine making industry was a slow-moving, traditional affair and Tony knew that patience would be his most vital commodity if he was to make it a success. It would take time, but he hoped that one day he could add his name to such historic wine making families as Lamont, Cabonivic, Talijanich, Pineli and Kosivich.

Tony's wife, Mandy, was in her own corner of the office studiously going through the books, occasionally blowing the fringe from her face in exasperation at the relative small turnover the winery was making. This was not what she was used to. Tony had met her at a party held by Saatchi and Saatchi five years ago. Back then she was an ambitious sales rep who effortlessly held her own in what was a predominantly male dominated environment. When they met the last thing they were looking for was a serious relationship. She was a determined career girl who was making her way up the advertising ladder. He had just come out of a sad marriage and had vowed never to get into a relationship with a woman ever again. They were friends at first, but gradually became close and eighteen months later they packed their old lives away to make a fresh new start together in Oz.

Tony squinted towards the west side of the winery and saw a familiar figure walking through one of the paths. His business partner, Jake, was ambling his considerable frame up towards the office. Tony picked up the phone, put it on loud speaker and quickly called his number.

"Git yer fat arse up here an make me a coffee," Tony laughed as he saw his friend look each way, then towards the office.

"Oi've gotta better oidea," Jake said in his thick Australian brogue, as he grabbed his crotch and turned towards Tony at the window. "Why don't ya get ya wife to lick me dick, Costello, you mangy Scottish Prick."

Tony howled with laughter and shrugged his shoulders towards Mandy who just shook her head, so used she was to their playful boyish banter.

"Alright, Sophie, love, how the devil are ya?" Jake asked as he planted a big wet kiss on Mandy's cheek. He was perspiring heavily under his loose khaki suit. Although this was Australia's winter time, it was unseasonably mild outside.

"So tell me, love," Jake went on conspiratorially to Mandy, just loud enough for Tony to hear. "What on Jesus' name are you doing married to that mongrel?" he asked winking towards Tony. "I mean, I suppose he does possess some of that Anglo-Celtic-Italian charm, but let's face it love, he's as ugly as a hat full of arseholes!" Jake laughed as he collapsed onto the new leather settee.

"Well it definitely ain't for his money if these figures are anything to go by!" Mandy said pointing to a document she had been studying.

"Och, no worries!" Jake boomed across the room. "Once the summer time's here, those dopey yanks will be flooding this place with wallets stuffed with green stuff, and we'll be laughing all the way to the bank."

Whilst Mandy and Jake discussed the merits of the latest business figures, Tony was staring out the window seemingly in another world. Mandy and Jake looked at each other cautiously. They both knew what was laying heavily on his mind.

"Ehm you ah, you heard from the boy?" Jake asked quietly.

"Not yet," Tony said blankly. The boy they were talking about was Steven, Tony's son. He still lived in Motherwell where he was brought up. When Mandy and Tony came over to Australia, they all agreed it was best that Steven stay and try to finish his exams. Tony felt at the time it was a good idea, but hadn't taken into consideration what effect it would have on his only son. They had a funny relationship. His mother, Tony's wife, had walked out on both of them when Steven was still young. This would normally bring a father and son closer, but Tony and Steven just seemed to drift on like nothing had happened. It frustrated Tony that he couldn't get closer to the boy and he was ashamed to say that he felt a sense of relief when the Australian adventure put some space between them.

Now, though, two things had happened that made Tony regret leaving his son behind. The first was the suicide of Clare Murray, Jack's daughter. Tony and Jack and known each other a long time and he was devastated when he heard the news. It wasn't until he managed to get a hold of Jack to offer his condolences that he found that Steven had been romantically involved with Clare. Jack had assured Tony that Steven was ok and he had in fact involved himself with Jack and his campaign team. Tony was glad to hear this. Not just because Steven was putting his undoubted intelligence to good use, but that in his absence he had Jack to help and guide him. This had given Tony a calming peace of mind and he began to feel more relaxed about his son being on his own in Scotland.

Yesterday all that changed. At around eight o'clock yesterday morning he received a phone call. At first he couldn't make out the person on the other line. About a year ago he had been trying to contact Steven who'd left him a few numbers he could try and reach him at. One of them was a lady called Patricia who was the mother of Lisa, Steven's flatmate. They got talking and Tony was moved by how much concern she seemed to have for his son. After a brief chat, Tony gave her his home number, asking her to phone him if there was anything about Steven she felt he had to know. He hadn't heard from her again until yesterday. Patricia had told Tony the desperately sad news about Gary, Steven's best friend. When she told him what had happened he felt like he had just been run over by a freight train. Gary, young Gary Stubbs, dead? It couldn't possibly be. Out of all the friends of Steven's who came round to the house Gary Stubbs was easily his favourite. An old man cut short, he used to think.

Tony remembered the time he was laying slabs out on the back garden. He had asked Steven to make himself available in case he needed a hand. When he appeared, he had brought three of his friends with him, Gerry, Eddie and Gary.

"Hi, Dad," Steven said with as much enthusiasm as he could muster.

"Eh hello, Mr Costello," Eddie and Gerry said in nervous unison.

"Tony boy, whit's happenin'?" Gary said taking his jacket off, gearing himself for a hard shift.

And what a shift he put in. The other boys tried gamefully to help, but by the end they were, at best, getting in the way. Gary, on the other hand, was lifting and laying, cutting and measuring like a seasoned tradesman. When he went into the fridge and helped himself to a beer, Tony could hardly deny him it.

"Well, you know how I feel," Mandy said, trying to keep her emotions in check. Tony rolled his eyes towards Jake; both of them had been through this conversation before.

"And don't make that face Tony, you know I'm right. You should never have left him. He was sixteen for God's sake, sixteen years of age, and now he's having to deal with all this and we can't even be there for him?" Mandy's voice began to crack with emotion. She was very fond of Steven. When Tony introduced them he never made her feel uneasy or unwelcome. They shared the same taste in books and music and when they left for Australia she was heartbroken.

"We'll get im over here, get some proper Aussie beer dhan his throat," Jake roared, lifting the mood. Tony looked at these two very different people. They were his family, his rock, his circle. He wanted Steven to be part of that circle; wanted it more than anything.

In Motherwell's large, draughty Cathedral, a lone Gothic coffin sat squarely in front of the impressive symmetrical altar. This time tomorrow night the body that lay in the coffin would be put to rest in Airbles cemetery. But for those who knew the young man, and knew the love and pride he had for his home town, his spirit would always remain in the adjoining Orbiston Street, a place of magic and romance, that he felt more than anyone ever did.

CHAPTER 17

FUNERAL FOR A FRIEND

ALL I CAN SEE IS A SHADOW... A PERSON, a real... no. Shadow... out, out, in, in, shadow... in.

Jack's helping me to bed. My limp body can offer no resistance. It doesn't want to... be here? Yes. No.

I can't make sense of anything. I remember Lisa. Definitely remember Lisa. Gary, naw, naw not Gary... no, no tears. Out, out, in... shadow coming, tears real tears, unlike me... no-tears Stevie. Her mam, a taxi... gone.

Jack came next. Tried to talk to me. Told me to let it all out, you'll be ok. I'm here, for you Steven, I'm here for you always.

Lisa.

Shock... no Gary, no Gary, my, my... who's Gary? Tears. Real, real tears, unlike me, Costello... I cry no tears... cocodemol, sleep, dream sleepsleepsleep.

Jack's standing in front of me pulling my black tie this way, then that. I had a rough sleep, mad, mad dreams. Clare, Stubbsy. Too much death in such a short time. I've never felt anything like this before. The mornings are the worst. I wake up thinking the world is the same as it was and that he is still here. Then it hits me... bang! He's gone, Stubbsy's dead, he's not coming back. When Clare committed suicide I was able to rationalize my feeling towards it because I knew that she was in control of her destiny. Just like my mum and dad. They had left me sure, but they did it on their own terms. It meant I could channel any anger and resentment towards them directly. I had a target for my resentment. But with Stubbsy, it's different. He didn't want to go, didn't want to die.

I still can't believe I'm talking about him in the past tense. I remember the night out we had in Glasgow a few months back. He told me he wouldn't leave me the way the others did. And he meant it. I know he did and it made me feel good. He was the closest person to me in the world and I don't know what I am going to do without him.

Thank God for Jack. He came for me after I had told Lisa. He took me in and looked after me. What have I done to deserve the attention of such a wonderful man? He's here with me now. He's attending the funeral, which makes thing easier for me. At Clare's funeral I was standing on my own, exposed, and the thought of going through that again terrifies me. I'm worried about Lisa. She has taken the big man's death badly. She was obviously in love with him. Obvious now, but not obvious before. Yet, despite her pain, I envy her. The ability, that is in no way unique to her, to openly grieve, to cry loud painful tears, how I wish that... I could well... somehow, go to that place. To weep and to mourn openly. Crying is such a cleansing affair and I wish to God I could go there, but, despite myself, I can't. I'm left with a numbness of the soul, and an ache in my stomach that I can't let out. I hope Lisa will be ok.

Peter Cairns, of the Cathedral St Vincent De Paul, quickly stuffed the 'punter pull out' from this morning's *Daily Record* into his pocket as Father Delaney approached the entrance of the tabernacle. He was eyeing potential winners for the big meeting at Wolverhampton. He had been following the form of a horse from A. Smart's stable in Lanark. Peter couldn't contain his excitement when he saw that the horse was the only one Smart had taken to the meeting. It was called 'Mother's Keeper' and was steadying its price at 22/1. Peter knew only too well that an experienced stableman like Smart wouldn't take just one horse all the way down to Wolverhampton if he didn't think it was capable of doing the business.

"Good morning, Peter, and how are we this morning?" Father Delaney asked in his soft, lilting Cork accent.

"I am doin' fine, Father. Everything is set up for this morning's service Father. The pews are fairly filling up, I think it could be a busy one," Peter mused.

"Yes, they often are," Father Delaney sighed, "such a tragic waste of a young life. I was with the family last night, such fine people, completely devastated, as you can imagine."

Peter nodded solemnly.

"Any winners for today, Peter?" Father Delaney asked, nodding towards the crudely disguised racing pull out hanging from the back of Peter's jacket pocket.

"Eh och naw Father, just a wee flutter, a bit of fun, ye know?" Peter stammered feeling himself blush furiously.

"Ah well, be sure to be making a gesture towards the upkeep of the church should the Lord see fit to be smiling some luck you way, Peter," Father Delaney said mischievously, laughing to himself.

"Of course, Father, of course," Peter said as he bowed his head and made his way to the church entrance.

The choir sang an echoing rendition of 'Star of the Sea' as Father Delaney was led through the chapel by two young altar girls. The place was packed out. In fact, he hadn't seen the place so busy. At the top left of the church was a sea of purple blazers from the school the young man had attended. There were people of all ages, faiths and religion. Jack Murray, the MSP for Motherwell and Wishaw, was in attendance. All were here to pay respects to a young man so cruelly taken from this world.

EDDIE

Eddie looked left then right. Where the fuck was Gerry? He hated coming to these places on his own. He was convinced churches, or chapels as the Tims called them, were designed solely for the purpose of installing abject fear into his soul. He hated the Gothic depictions and was now convinced they were telling some kind of story that didn't end well for the Jesus fella.

Big Stubbsy. Eddie still couldn't comprehend it. He wasn't one to show his emotions and the thought of breaking down in front of all these people terrified him. He became quite teary last night in his bedroom as he remembered the old times with Stubbsy; times, which now, more than ever, seemed so far away. He first met him when he was in the third year at school.

GERRY

Fuckin well greetin aw night, by the way. Big Fuckin Stubbsy? Fuckin deed. Car crash. Still cannae believe it. Jist keep thinkin' about him, win we wir wains, in that. The first day at school. I don't remember anything aboot it, the class or teacher or that. But I do remember big Stubbs. He walks intae the class and there's nae seats left. Noo, maist wains that age wid just turn round in start greetin'. No Stubbsy bit. He just swaggers up and planks ehsel on the teacher's chair, simple as ye like. Ah mind the look oan his face when we aw stertit laughin, ewis jist sittin' there as if tae say "An whit? Sa fuckin chairm so it is."

Whit a laugh. Whit a boy.

Chapel's mobbed huns in everythin'. Where's that daft cunt Eddie? There's Stevie up the tap wi the family. Cannae face sittin' wae him though. If am honest av never really liked Stevie. Ewis bashin oan about how shite Motherwell is in aw that. Fair do's, bit he stay there an aw, if ay disnae like he knows whit ay cin dae. Ah mind wan night, me in Stubbs were huvin' a scoop doon Daniels, few gemmes a snooker in at.

Ah says tae the big man, "Fuckin yon Stevie, whit's wae ow this politics shite?" The big man jist pure growls at me, knuckles gaun aw white round the cue. Ah jist pits the hied doon in splits the reds. Ah suppose if onyhin good's come oot aw this situation is that ah'll no need tae hing aboot wi that pretentious prick Costello, whilst aw the time kiddin' on ah dig the guy no? Still, Big Fuckin Stubbsy, by the way, cannae fuckin get our it.

WEE RYAN FARRELL

Wee Ryan Farrell took a quick look round at the mass of people in the church and let the huge, heart-draining tears, which had been building up since he woke this morning, flow openly from his bloodshot eyes. He was attending the first funeral of his young life and the pain was becoming too much to bear. Ryan was in no doubt as to what he had lost. There were those in attendance who had lost a son. Others, a brother or friend. For Ryan though, he had lost the closest thing he ever had to a father. Ever since the day Stubbsy saved him from the clutches of Porky O'Rourke, he had mentored him in everything life had to offer.

As he looked around the chapel, it was clear that it wasn't just he who had been touched by his electrical tutor. The first thing he noticed was the birds. They all looked so hot in their black two-piece suits, crying as they did so softly into small, white handkerchiefs. Despite himself, he imagined them all as ex-lovers of Stubbsy's, all having had him so fleetingly in their lives, heartbroken that they would never have him again. He checked himself though. They were probably just like him. Sorrowed that someone who meant so much had been taken from them so soon.

Ryan played back last night one more time in his head. On Saturday night he had left Starka early after he indulged in a heart to heart with Jade. He was feeling tired and emotional after what had happened to Stubbsy and took advantage of Jade's sympathetic ear. He awoke on the Sunday with a horrible feeling of dread. How on earth would Jade want to go out with a blubbering idiot like him? He didn't have to wait long for the answer. To his unbridled excitement she had come round to his mum's last night to see how he was. It was the first time he had been in her company sober. At first he was nervous, but after a while he relaxed and they both spent the night talking about everything and nothing. He took the initiative and asked her out on a proper date and she had said yes. Ryan knew deep down that someone, somewhere would have been very proud of him.

LISA

Lisa mournfully waited and eventually moved after the sea of black-clothed people that uniformly followed the pall bearers and selected family members who had been nominated to carry the coffin out of the church towards the hearse that would eventually take Gary's body to its resting place in Airbles cemetery. Her mother was by her side, holding her tightly. She was sobbing, lightly remarking on how it had been a lovely mass. And it had been, Lisa thought. The priest tried as best he could to sum up Gary's life in the designated hour that he had at his disposal. Everyone laughed and cried at the appropriate times and would soon be toasting his name in different pubs up and down the town.

For Lisa though, she found herself channelling her raw pain and anger at an unlikely source. All through the mass people showed their emotions in different ways. Older men bit their top lips and forced their emotions deep down, whilst the women saved their grief for the end of the mass, crying in silent dignity. This was in contrast to the young people in attendance. This was the generation of Big Brother and David Beckham. Crying was as natural as breathing. Both male and female unashamedly sobbed their way through the service with no thought of how they may look to others. But Lisa had noticed that one person in attendance was showing no sign of grief at all. No tears, no shake of the head. Just a blank stare throughout the mass. There was a time when his ice cold debonair impressed her, but now it angered her more than anything in the world. Who did he think he was? Did he think he was too cool to show emotion? Was he looking down on her and the rest for openly grieving for their friend? The thought enraged her to the point she decided she could not go to the cemetery or to any gathering afterwards. She was afraid of what she might say, afraid she might let it out... no, no she couldn't do that. Instead of heading for the cemetery, she ambled her way down Orbiston Street and thought about the promises she intended to honour and the feelings she could no longer keep inside.

THE CHOPPER

The mass was over and the horrible bit down at Airbles had passed. Now it was the time I hated the most. I'm in the Chopper wi' Eddie and Gerry and some more friends and relatives beginning the obligatory post-funeral bevy session. Old stories are being told with the same vigour as the pints are being sank. I'm not feeling it. They are all good guys I suppose, but the one person I want to speak to isn't here. In fact, she was nowhere to be seen at the cemetery or the steak pie nosh up in St Bride's Hall.

"Eddie, you seen Lisa?" I shout to Eddie over the noise, which seems to be getting louder.

"No seen her, Stevie boy. She was at the mass though," Eddie said helpfully, which didn't help at all.

"Lisa, wee blonde hing, tidy?" one of Stubbsy's uncles shouts towards me.

"Aye, you seen her?"

"Aye, she went straight oot the chapel and took a left towards the steelworks," he said.

Orbiston Street. Of course. The poor wee thing's took this bad. I better go find her.

"Gerry, ahm away tae find wee Lisa, ah'll see ye in a bit," I said to Big Gerry as I put my suit jacket on.

"Eh aye whatever," he says rolling his eyes towards a few guys in his company. Whit's wrang wi him?

The rain is beating down as I make my way up towards Orbiston Street. I walk its full length, past the bingo and the back end of the police station. I am about to give up my search when, just as I reach the underpass that funnels you out towards the brew office, I see her. She's sitting on a little brick wall on her own, totally oblivious to the thundering rain lashing down upon her.

"Hey you, what you doing out here in the rain?" I say as I wipe the rain from my face. She looks at me blankly then turns away.

"Lisa, are you ok?" I say as I try to put my arm around her.

"Fuck off, just fuck off and leave me alone!" she screams at me, pushing my arm away.

"Lisa, what's wrong?" I ask her. She looks demented and has a look of contempt in her eye that I've never seen before.

"What's wrong? Are you for real? Is that what this is all about, Stevie? Do you not actually live in the real world?" She looks away and begins to cry.

"Lisa what's going on?" She looks up at me for a second then lunges towards me, kicking and screaming.

"You bastard, you absolute bastard. Your best friend is dead and you think you're above grief. You think you're better than the rest of us. Mr Stevie am-too-cool–to-cry Costello. You're pathetic, ah hate you, AH HATE YOU!"

At first I'm stunned, then I begin to realise what she has said to me. The anger that is rising inside me explodes.

"Who the fuck are you, ay? One wee fumble in the town wi Stubbsy and you think you can tell me how to grieve for my best friend. Aw poor wee Lisa, her mam's her gran and her sister's her mam! Boo the fuck hoo. At least you know your parents. My mother and father are gone, ah've never had them, NEVER, FUCKIN NEVER, LISA!" She's crying into her lap now as I scream this abuse in her direction. "When you've buried your girlfriend and best friend within a year of each other come back and lecture me, but until then you can fuck off."

Lisa looks up at me coldly, shakes her head. "Ah can't take this anymore Stevie."

I take a deep breath. "Take what Lisa, what are you talking about?"

"The lies, ah can't take the lies anymore," she says staring into the distance.

"Lisa what are talking about," I ask anxiously.

"Clare," she says.

I feel a jolt strike straight through me. I grab her by her lapels.

"What are you talking about... TELL ME, FUCKING TELL ME?"

She looks towards the sky. The rain is slamming against her face. From a distance there's a rumbling of thunder. The wind is furiously blowing against us. Lisa looks me straight in the eye.

"Ahm sorry, so, so sorry."

"Sorry for what, Lisa, what are ye talking about?" I plead with her.

"It's Clare, Stevie," she said.

All of sudden all the noise and chaos around us disappears. It's only her and I.

"Stevie, Clare's still alive."

CHAPTER 18

DEATH OF THE GOWKTHRAPPLE DREAM

Any half-decent self-help book will tell you that the cornerstone of one's ability to maintain happiness and a degree of self-worth is to Be Positive. You lose your job. Be Positive. Your mum's passed away? Be Positive. Your wife's a lesbian and is leaving you for that German Zumba instructor? Try and Be Positive.

Amanda didn't read self-help books. Her job prospects were on the up after being given a full-time contract with Scottish Power. She had never set foot in a gym, let alone gone to a Zumba class and, the last time she checked, her mum was in rude health. The only thing Amanda wanted in her life right now was to be negative. Unfortunately for her though, what can't speak, can't lie. It was there in the NHS North

Lanarkshire letter that had arrived last week. Amanda was positive. HIV positive.

If she was honest, she knew it was coming. Although she was three days, two weeks and eleven months clean of heroin, it seemed her derelictions of the past had finally caught up with her. It was a good idea at the time, she thought. Two years after she had given birth to her beautiful little girl Amie, her idyllic world had fallen apart. She met Amie's father when she had been on a night out with friends in the Blue Rupee in Hamilton. Ahmer was from the Bhopal region in the Indian state of Madhya. He was the manager of a restaurant, one of a small chain owned by his family. Amanda, who at thirty-one years old was feeling frustratingly single, was coy to his obvious initial flirtations, but eventually found herself falling for his soft, good looks and polite Indian charm. They went out on a date the following week and soon became inseparable.

At first, Ahmer was everything Amanda wanted in a man. He was kind, considerate, thoughtful and loyal. He was very committed to his family and Amanda was delighted when he said that his dream was to one day start a family of his own. Amanda, along with her only other sibling, Michael, had been brought up by her mother, Dorothy, after their father had left them when they were still in primary school. Dorothy was a loud, hardworking woman who didn't suffer fools. Unfortunately, she also had a succession of failed relationships and Amanda's childhood was littered with periods where she had to try and pick up the pieces after another man failed to live up to her mother's inexplicably high expectations.

After only six months of dating Amanda fell pregnant. Although it came as a shock, she couldn't wait to have Ahmer's baby and spend the rest of her life with him. But as Amanda went through the normal stages of pregnancy, Ahmer began to change too. He insisted she move into his home in Overtown that he shared with his parents and two older brothers. In the house they would all talk in their native language and the brothers and father ignored her completely. Amanda felt more and more isolated as the weeks passed. Ahmer himself had become moody and aggressive. He barred her from seeing her friends and went ballistic if he heard her speaking on the phone to any of her family. He had also become prone to leaving for India at short notice. Any time Amanda asked why he was spending so much time there, he would scream at her to stop asking so many questions. Amanda was feeling helpless. Despite the best effort of her mother to try and persuade her to leave "that Paki bastard" she clung on, hoping that by the time the baby came things would be different.

About a month before she was due to give birth Amanda awoke to find that the house was empty, bar Ahmer's second oldest brother, Shamal. When she asked where everyone was Shamal just looked at her, then turned away and laughed. Later that day, when she was lying resting, Shamal came into her room to see her. He sat down next to her and inappropriately began to rub his finger up and down her arm.

"He has gone home to get married. You do know that, don't you?" Shamal leered.

"What? Don't be daft, we're having a baby for God's sake!" Amanda said, a wave of anxiety washing over her.

"Ha, you daft, wee Scottish lassies, you don't have clue, man," Shamal said in his crude broken Scottish accent that Amanda had always hated.

"He has been preparing to marry this girl since he was twelve. Ahmer is the jewel in the family crown; do you honestly think he would give all that up to marry you? He is a man of honour who will do anything for this family. I, on the other hand…" At this point Shamal slipped his hand in between Amanda's legs and tried to kiss her. Despite being heavily pregnant, Amanda whacked the side of Shamal's face and struggled towards the door. She walked out to the main road and flagged down a taxi to her mother's.

Five weeks later Amanda gave birth to her daughter, Amie. It had been a tough time, but with the help of her family she slowly began to get her life back together. One Saturday afternoon, a few weeks after Amie was born, Ahmer phoned her mobile and left a voicemail.

"Amanda, I want to apologise for everything I've done to you. I know there is no way you can forgive me but I would like to one day see the baby. I know this will take some time, but she is my daughter and I don't want to abandon her. In the meantime, I will put money in your account every week to help with her upbringing."

And he did. Four hundred pounds every week, without fail. Although at first Amanda was reluctant to take his money, it meant she didn't have to go out and work and instead could spend some vital quality time with her beautiful daughter. After some months, relations between Amanda and Ahmer had thawed. She didn't have any feelings for him, but wasn't adverse to him playing a part in Amie's life. He was married now and expecting another child.

To begin with Ahmer had access to Amie every second weekend. This increased to every weekend once Amanda was happy with his intentions. Everything was fine, until one weekend Ahmer asked about the likelihood of flying Amie down to London to visit family he had down there. Amanda, who had been impressed with his commitment towards Amie, both financially and emotional, could see no harm in this. The next day she took Amie to Tesco in Wishaw, paid for five pictures, and applied for her first passport.

On the Sunday of Ahmer and Amie's trip to London, Amanda waited patiently at her mother's house for her beloved baby's return. Things had been looking up. She had started working part-time with Scottish Power in East Kilbride. The job itself was tedious, but the people she worked with were nice enough and it was good to get out of her mother's house. She had applied for a home of her own with the council, but had so far only been offered the tower blocks in Muirhouse and Gowkthrapple. As a single mother, she knew that if she waited she would be offered better.

Ahmer was due home at eight o'clock. By half-past eight there was no sign of him. Amanda was feeling a little uneasy, but assumed his flight must have been delayed. When it got to ten o'clock Amanda began to panic. That panic turned to sheer terror when she phoned Glasgow Airport to see if there had been a delay, only to be told that there was only one flight coming from any airport in London that day and it had landed on time seven hours ago. Amanda's mum phoned the police whilst Amanda drove to Ahmer's parents. When she got there she frantically banged on every door and window, demanding someone come out and speak to her. Although she could see a silhouette of Ahmer's mother, no one came to the door.

Back at the house a sympathetic police officer said they were treating Amanda's nightmare as a missing person and would stretch the search worldwide. He advised them that they must engage with the press and put pressure on the Indian consulate to help them. There was, however, no need. At twelve o'clock Ahmer's father came round to the house to give Amanda as much information as he could.

"Amie is alive and well. She is with Ahmer and his family in Bhopal. We have had other family members verify this and are, as we speak, trying to talk Ahmer into bring the little girl home. We knew nothing of his intentions and are absolutely furious with our son. I give you my word that we will do everything we can to make sure your daughter is returned safely."

Over the next few days and weeks there had been no sign of Ahmer and Amie. The police were in constant contact with the Indian officials, who said there was nothing they could do as Ahmer's name was on her passport and there had been no restriction placed on him. They were in no position to send him and Amie home. This had left Amanda devastated. For weeks she was in a trance. Unable to work, eat or sleep. Her relationship with her mother, who blamed her for letting Ahmer take Amie away in the first place, had broken down. Because of this Amanda made a decision that would, in time, prove fatal. She phoned the council and accepted the offer of a flat in the rundown area of Gowtherapple.

Within a week she had begun to drink heavily. Since she moved in she had only left to go to the local shop for some groceries and cheap vodka, which she used to numb the pain of being apart from her baby. One night someone knocked on Amanda's door. When she went to the door, a slightly stoned guy was at the door with a plate of muffins.

"Eh awrite hen, am, eh Milky, fae next door no," he said as he handed Amanda the muffins he had baked for her earlier. "A wee movin in gift fae the Milkster, a gesture ay warmth and friendship that one hopes will lay the foundations of a everlasting friendship."

Despite his unkempt appearance Amanda was drawn to Milky's big, kind eyes. Although she had never met him, she felt comfortable enough to invite him in and share her vodka. When she began to tell him everything that had happened to her and the unbearable pain she was in, Milky thought nothing of offering her a smoke of something that had a history of taking away the pain.

"Here, wee bit a kit, unsafe in the hands of Gowky's less desirable members ay the neighbourhood watch, but harmless recreational when enjoyed in the safe boundaries set out by the Right Honourable Milky," he said. "Take away the pain, just like that." It sounded good.

Amanda took the tinfoil from Milky and inhaled as much as she could. It caught the back of her throat and made her cough violently. At first she felt dizzy and sick, the same way she had when she'd smoked cannabis for the one and only time when she was a teenager. Suddenly she felt all floaty and dream-like. All her cares seemed to drift into the distance. She reached out, she tried to touch her fears, her pain, but she couldn't. They were gone, gone... gone.

Doctor Logan had assured Amanda that the current advancement in modern medicine meant that HIV was no longer a life sentence and that she could live a perfectly happy life, if she was vigilant with her medicine. She knew deep down though that medication wasn't the answer. As she looked around her small, newly refurbished flat that she had worked hard to convert, she knew she had made a mess of her life.

After her first taste of heroin, Milky had come round the next day to make sure she was ok. "A wee toke noo, Amanda, one wee skelp. That's aw that wis. Nae mair tho, yer a good lassie an ye need tae be strong fir yer wane in at. Noo ahm awiy fir ah bit, so keep it cool and take it easy ok?"

Amanda nodded, but she knew she was going to take smack again. The next night she hooked up with Arlene and her man from the flat upstairs. She knew her from school and knew she was a habitual drug taker. That night there was no tin foil, just cold steel needles.

For the next two months she had heroin party after heroin party with Arlene and the rest of her junky mates. Sharing needles like they shared old stories. All Amanda wanted to do was not think about the grief that was engulfing her soul. All this changed though, one wet Tuesday morning when Amanda awoke in her dingy flat shivering and in need of some more drugs. She wasn't quite at desperate addict stage yet, but she was getting there. As she drew back her curtain to let some light in, she saw something that made her heart jump through her pasty skin. No heroin withdrawal was strong enough to cancel out the joy of what was unfolding in front of her eyes. Ahmer's dad was struggling with a baby bag and buggy. In his right arm was a little child who had changed so much, yet hadn't changed at all. It was Amie! Ahmer had come to his senses and brought her home.

For the next few weeks, Amanda concentrated on getting clean and re-bonding with her little girl. Her relationship with her mother had broken down completely and she found that old friends were not as reliable as they used to be. Thankfully, she had Milky. Even though he still used heroin – amazing Amanda with his ability to use and still live a normal life – he helped her through the heroin detox and was very handy when it came to decorating the flat. She had found a true friend.

Now though, everything had changed for the worse again. Her mother wanted no more to do with her and she was sure that if she died, Ahmer would get full custody of Amie and take her back to India. There was only one hope, one chance. She hadn't known Clare Murray long, but Amanda felt that she was all she had. Clare was confident and vivacious. Clare had major problems of her own. However, more importantly to Amanda, Clare had a plan.

CHAPTER 19

LANDSLIDE '97 (THINGS CAN ONLY GET BETTER)

"Whit da fuck ye oan aboot 'plan'? Whit fuckin plan? Have you lost yer mind Lisa, seriously? This is sick!" Stevie barked aggressively.

Lisa shook her head and took a swift gulp of her Southern Comfort and lemonade. After revealing to Stevie that his dead ex-girlfriend was actually still alive, he had dragged her to the Bullfrog pub; a pub so-old fashioned in both decor and ambience that only two years ago, Lisa, because she was female, would not have been allowed on the premises.

"Stevie, ah know this is hard for you to take in and when ah tell you what really happened, you will believe it even less. All ah want from you is to listen to me and ah promise ah'll tell you everything ah know."

Stevie looked at her sceptically, but eventually waved his hand, motioning Lisa to continue.

"Ok," Lisa sighed. "It all began about six months before Clare disappeared..."

THE PLAN

"You, you can't be a serious, Clare," Amanda stuttered, struggling to come to terms with what Clare had just told her. "You... we... it will never work, Clare, it's outrageous. How could we get away with it?"

"Then ah'll get arrested, and Amie will be on the first flight to India to spend the rest of her life with her psycho father. Let's face it though, Amanda, you're HIV positive, you're going to die. If we sit back and do nothing that is what's going to happen anyway. This way? Well, this way, at least we have a chance."

Amanda first met Clare when she was trying to gain some political leverage from her father, Jack, after Amie had been taken to India by her father without her consent. Jack Murray was overtly sympathetic to

Amanda's case. He promised her he would do everything in his power to make sure her baby girl was brought home safely. Amanda left Jack's office feeling elated. Having a man of his political standing in her corner would have to make a difference. For the first time since Ahmer had disappeared with Amie, she had hope that she would see her daughter again.

A week later, a visit from Clare left Amanda totally deflated. When she opened the door to her, the first thing Amanda noticed was that Clare had the same unkempt, brown bushy hair that she had. She had a warm smile and, although her attire was understated to say the least, she exuded a sense of her own style and self-worth, and everything she said had such a determined steely resolve to it that you couldn't help believe it. Clare explained to Amanda that, despite her father's assurances, there was very little he could do. Jack Murray was inextricably linked to the Asian community and had fought their corner in Parliament on many occasions. Clare explained that although her father was sympathetic to her cause, his hands were tied and there was little he could do to help her. This sent Amanda into an even deeper depression. For her part, Clare promised to do everything she could to help. She was characteristically true to her word.

Over the following few months they became close friends. Clare helped Amanda through the despair of not having her little girl at home, her decline into drug abuse and subsequent re-acquaintance with her daughter. When Amanda was diagnosed HIV positive,

Clare was a tower of strength, helping her seek the best medical advice and counselling to help her deal with such a life-changing situation. For Clare's part, she found in Amanda a true friend. She was drawn to her innocence, which at times was her downfall, and felt a need to protect her from the world that had been treating her so badly for the most part of her life. And with little Amie, she felt a maternal instinct fire within her that she never knew existed before. It was this natural instinct that had driven her to devise the plan that she was now presenting to a bewildered Amanda.

"So let me get this straight. Ah take my own life, in your car, in your clothes, with a suicide note to this Stevie guy, written by you?" Amanda said, glaring seriously at Clare.

"Yes, that's correct," Clare said with a firm determination that Amanda had grown used to.

"And then what?" Amanda asked weakly, as though she was resigned to this mad plan already.

"You write your mum a letter. You tell her you are going to America to start a new life and not to try and contact you. You give me your passport, birth certificate, driver's licence, bank statements, credit cards, everything that identifies you. Ah make myself look as much like your passport photo as possible, which you know won't be hard, ah take Amie to the airport and we fly to the States and never ever come back," Clare said, staring blankly at Amanda.

Amanda took a deep breath. Once she had gained her composure she looked Clare in the eye and slowly began to speak.

"Ok, so we know why this is a good plan for Amie and ah, but what about you? Clare, ah know you have not been telling me everything," Amanda said taking Clare by the hand firmly. "Clare, if you want me to go through with this you have to tell me the truth. You are clearly running away from something and ah want you to tell me what it is."

Clare put her hands on her head and pulled great mounds of hair away from her eyes. She was about to tell someone what had actually happened that night. The night that had plagued her thoughts and dreams ever since.

3ʳᵈ MAY 1997

CLARE CEREMONIOUSLY PULLED THE OASIS POSTER off her wall in one sweeping move. Their last album had been a disappointment and she found herself being seduced by the more seductive tones of bands such as Spiritualized, The Verve and a new band from Leeds called Embrace. She was impressed at the fearless way they approached the subject of love and love lost. She swooned at Danny's tender lyrics in 'Fireworks', sang at the top of her voice along with Richard to 'The Drugs Don't Work', and cried herself to sleep with Jason and 'Broken Heart'. She hoped that one day there would be some skinny, indie kid with a guitar who would write such an emotive song about her. At the age of fifteen she was mature enough to know that love was more than just sweet melodies and beautiful lyrics. She just wanted one song, though, to be about her; it was all she ever dreamed about.

'Yessss! Goodbye Portillo, you Tory bastard!' Clare heard the muffled cheers come from downstairs, where the party had being going on for over two hours now. She had been up at Wishaw Sports Centre to watch Frank Roy romp home to win the candidacy for Motherwell and Wishaw. Although this was pretty much expected, it was what was going on in the rest of the country that was causing the most excitement. Labour, led by an invigorated Tony Blair, were heading for a historic landslide victory. This was monumental for Clare and her family. Her dad was a popular figure in the Scottish Labour Party and was seen as the ideal candidate to represent Motherwell and Wishaw in a Scottish Parliament, if and when the new government delivered its promise of devolution. She knew that tonight's win was everything Jack Murray had dreamed of. She remembered election nights from the past when the joy of winning the seat locally was tempered by yet another crushing defeat by the Tories. She was happy for her dad tonight and believed he deserved to enjoy it as much as anyone.

Clare had always felt a closeness to her father that went beyond the 'daddy's little princess' relationship. They were like friends almost. They liked the same music and films, watched the same TV programmes and shared the same sense of humour. This meant that her mother was always on the outside, looking in. She always seemed to be in the background, shaking her head as Jack and Clare shared a joke or convulsed in fits of laughter whilst watching a comedy programme they both liked. Because of this, her relationship with her mother was strained, to say the least. She rarely fell out with her mother, like other girls her age often did, but there was no closeness, no real bonding. She didn't care though; her relationship with her father more than made up for it.

As the night went on, there were more cheers of victory. Clare could hear different people come and go. Just as she was about to turn over and try to get to sleep over all the noise, she heard someone tap on her door and enter her room.

"We did it Clare, hen, the Tories, Thatcher, Major, we wiped them out," Jack whispered as he sat down on

Clare's bed. Clare noticed something different about him. The kindness that usually exuded from his eyes was replaced with a steely glare that was almost leering. Then something happened that struck genuine fear into Clare's heart. Her dad took off his shoes, eased himself under her covers and held onto her head.

She could smell the whiskey and beer from his breath as he put his arms around her waist and pushed himself up towards her. She instantly felt scared and uncomfortable.

"Dad, ahm tired, please, ah want to sleep," but it was as if he couldn't hear her. His eyes were closed tight, almost like he didn't want to see what he was doing.

"You're so like your mother, Clare, yet something more, something special, my, my... you're mah special girl," he said slowly. She could feel his hands between her legs now. She could hear herself crying, but everything else was numb. She thought and hoped that she would pass out, but she didn't.

"My girl, mah special wee girl," he groaned as he took her pants down. He took his trousers off and she felt something poke against her, inside her. She tried to scream, but it was like a nightmare where you open your mouth and nothing comes out.

"It's just you and me baby, just you and me," he said as he manoeuvred himself into her. All the time his eyes were closed, almost like he couldn't look at what he was doing. After what seemed like a lifetime of excruciating pain, he finally stopped. He opened his eyes then quickly jumped out her bed, put on his trousers and went back down stairs to re-join the party. She could feel blood and goo all over her bed. She began to cry uncontrollably. Her perfect life, her youth, her innocence was leaving her. She put the cover over her and pretended to be asleep. Her bedroom door opened. She lifted one eye to see her Mum standing over her. She let out a small sniffle. Her mum could see she had been crying. She wanted her to come to her, to hold her and tell her everything would be ok. She didn't though. She just shook her head in disgust and walked out, leaving Clare with her tears and her pain.

Amanda looked at her friend with wild eyed anger and amazement. "Your… your… dad… Jack Murray… he… he… raped you?"

Clare composed herself and nodded. "Yeah, he did. Just once. Only that night, but yes, he raped me. Now ah don't want to go in to any more specifics, not just now anyway, but this is crucial to our plan being successful. My father has been tip-toeing around me for years. That night has never been mentioned since, but he knows if ah were ever to say anything, even though it would be my word against his, he would be finished. So when your body is eventually found, he will have to identify it. When he notices that the body isn't me, he will have sussed out what we have done. And since it will literally present him with a get out of jail card, he will go along with it and say that it *is* his daughter." Clare looked at Amanda with that steely determination in her eye again. "Amanda this plan *will* work. Now, you have to let me know, one hundred percent. Are you in?"

Amanda looked at this extraordinary individual before her. A girl with more guts and determination than anyone she had ever known. It was then that she realised that there was no one else she wanted her daughter to be brought up by.

"Ok Clare, ahm in."

CHAPTER 20

THE FALL

THE RAIN IS BLACK AND SO IS MY HEART so black black black Milky is here with a needle my needle he will inject the car the letter Clare Clare oh Clare please don't cry why Amie you must be strong for my Amie for now ah must leave ah must go Milky please inject inject please Amie ah will be with you always oh no Clare do not be afraid for ahm with you no more tears please don't cry Clare Clare your dad the rapist the bastard no more tears Milky please inject ahm falling black black goodbye black black black

"Ok it's done, it's over," Clare cried down the phone.

She and Milky had just pushed Amanda's body over the edge of the Cliff. Minutes before Milky had given her a lethal injection. She died instantly. And now, since they had to leave the car to authenticate the suicide, they had to wait for someone to come and pick them up.

"We're doing the right thing, aren't we Milky?" Clare said as they checked over the car one last time.

"Right, wrang, no really the issue noo is it? Jist gittin you an the wain ay that airport without anybody seein ye," Milky replied. "An yer flyin oot the night defo?"

"Yes, tonight. Hopefully my search party won't kick into action for a few days yet," Clare answered.

"Well you get yersel an the wain oan that plane an jist don't look back. Ah'll look after everything this side should anything go wrang. Clare, we've done the right thing," Milky said giving Clare a reassuring hug.

"Thank you, Milky, ah'll never forget you for what you have done, you are a special person," Clare said as tears began once again to well in her eyes.

"My pleasure. Just remember though, this is it, we can never speak again after this," Milky warned.

"Ah understand Milky, thank you."

One hour later a Fiat Punto driven by a young blonde girl pulled up and Milky and Clare drove off with her, leaving the car with the letter. The plan had been executed.

"So you took them to the airport?" Stevie said vacantly, as he fought to come to terms with everything Lisa had told him.

"Clare and ah became friends when you guys were going out," Lisa explained, trying to fight back her tears. "When she told me what she was going to do, she swore me to secrecy. If ah'd told you or anyone else about their plan it would have fallen through. Stevie, ah've carried this around with me for ages, it's been so hard lying to you, but ah didn't know what else to do."

Lisa wiped tears from her eyes. "Ah know this must be so difficult for you Stevie, finding out what Jack did, today of all days, but you have to see that this was the reason ah had to remain silent. How could ah ever tell anyone? How could ah do that, Stevie?"

Stevie sat quietly, occasionally rubbing his hand against his head.

"Say something Stevie, please?"

Stevie turned to Lisa and saw yet another friend he no longer knew.

"Lisa go home. Go home, pack all of your things, leave the flat and never contact me again."

She looked at him pleadingly through her tears which were now streaming down her face. "Please, Stevie, ah don't want to leave you, we need each other."

Stevie felt the anger rise from inside him. "NEED YOU? AH NEED YOU, FOR FUCK SAKE? LISA, YOU

ARE JUST THE SAME AS THE REST!" he roared at her across the table, causing some old punters to turn around startled.

"Eh you awrite, hen?" the barman inquired, looking suspiciously towards Stevie who didn't seem to hear him. Lisa gave the barman a small wave to let him know she was ok.

"YOU, MY MAM, MY DA, FUCKIN JACK, CLARE, EVEN WEE EDDIE AND GERRY, YOU'RE ALL THE FUCKIN SAME, YOU HAVE TREATED ME LIKE AM NOTHING, LIKE I DONT MATTER! I ONLY EVER HAD ONE PERSON, ONE, FRIEND, AND ONE FAMILY. AND HE'S SIX FOOT UNDER DOWN IN AIRBLES FUCKIN CEMETERY!"

Lisa howled a painful cry as she thought about Stubbsy. How had it come to this? She remembered only a few months back, her, Stevie and Stubbs. In Starka, the Tavern, the Beer Festival. They were happy then. Innocent even. Where had it all gone wrong? She finished her drink and stood to leave.

"Stevie, for what it's worth, ah only wanted to protect you," she said through her soft cries. "And I love you more than you'll know ever know, I am so very sorry for what I have done. Ah just hope that one day you will forgive me."

Stevie stared at the floor trying not to catch Lisa's eyes. She paused for a minute then made her way to the exit. Before leaving she turned round to look at Stevie. She remembered the good times and bad. He had been everything to her. Her mentor, her comrade, her confidant and her friend. Now though, as she left this shabby little pub on Shields Road, she knew she would never see him again.

Stevie gulped back his fifth pint of Guinness and took a sharp sip of the whiskey chaser that he had been putting off since his third pint. He was unaware of everything around him. He had no idea what time it was or how long he had been here. The dank bar was so aged in its decor you could be forgiven for thinking it was actually one of those retro seventies chic establishments that were popping up in Edinburgh and the West End of Glasgow. A quick look around and Stevie realised he was alone, apart from the old lady behind the bar and a wizened looking guy with a bunnet and walking stick who was sitting in the table directly in front of him. He hadn't noticed, but the man had been eagerly trying to catch Stevie's eye for the last half hour. When Stevie's gaze eventually met his, he lifted his half pint of heavy that was accompanied with the obligatory half measure and doffed his cap in Stevie's direction.

"Funeral, son?" the old man said, acknowledging Stevie's all-black attire.

"Aye man, Cathedral this morning," Stevie said drunkenly.

"Sad affairs, sad, sad affairs," the old man said wistfully. "Only last month, ah buried my dear friend, the legendary Hamish," the old man exclaimed, looking at Stevie for some recognition as to who the legendary Hamish was.

"Hamish?" Stevie raised an eyebrow.

"Hamish Imlach, Muirhouse's most celebrated son!" the old man announced. Stevie nodded and raised his glass. Although he wasn't up to speed with Imlach's work, he – like most people from these parts – had heard about Hamish Imlach. He was a famous folk singer who was friends with John Martin and Billy Connelly, both of whom had attended his funeral, and had written the beautiful Christy Moore song 'Black is the Colour'.

"Aye, ah fine man so eh wis. May ah?" the old man said as he took off his hat and placed it to his breast. Stevie wasn't quite sure what he was asking to be permitted to do but nodded in agreement all the same.

The old boy began a faultless rendition of Imlach's 'A Soldier's Prayer', followed by a more aggressive 'Erin Go Bragh' and finally a haunting 'Black Is the Colour'. The latter brought memories of Clare to the foremost of Stevie's muddled mind. Today he had learned of her lies, of Lisa and her betrayal and, darkly, of Jack, his political hero, whom he now knew was a sick paedophile rapist. After the old man with the walking stick had left, Stevie went to the bar for one last drink.

"Double Jameson's and ice, please," he slurred to the woman behind the bar who looked more like a head teacher. She raised her eyebrow, concerned at the obvious drunken state Stevie was in. He raised one finger to intimate he was only having one more. Reluctantly she poured his whiskey.

"A hard time for you son, the whole town was shocked by what happened. Ahm sorry about your friend," she said solemnly.

Stevie thought about this for a minute then said, "Aye, which one?" He gulped back his soft whiskey, left through the side door and walked into a dark, drizzly and unforgiving Muirhouse night.

CHAPTER 21

IF THIS AIN'T LOVE

THE SUN SHONE LIKE A BEACON ON THE EXHAUSTED holiday makers who had sporadically positioned themselves around the conventional, cool blue swimming pool. Its serene calmness was at odds with the psyche of those around it. They squinted their eyes, mechanically applied sun creams of varying levels of protection and sipped on cold local soft drinks, which had to be drunk in minutes before they lost their freshness, such was the ferocity of the heat that was emanating from the unforgiving sun. It was quiet now, yet somewhere in the distance, a hum of continental house music was playing continuously from a beach-side bar, broadcasting to everyone that the next party wasn't far away.

Most of them were nursing hangovers and drug-induced comedowns that were so intense some had to remind themselves that they were actually on holiday, a period of relaxation. However, the hangovers would soon dissipate. Around three o'clock they would timidly procure their first alcoholic drink of the day, which, initially, would be difficult to stomach, but would soon be flowing more freely. This would, in turn, re-ignite their desire for cheap drugs, even cheaper sex and a new night of sun-soaked, neon debauchery would commence.

"Fuckin roastin, Eddie, ma son!" Gerry sang as he opened the sliding doors of their apartment, in their standard hotel, in the east side of San Antonio bay.

They had arrived on the holiday island of Ibiza earlier that morning. After dumping their cases, they headed out to start what they hoped would be a week's worth of drugs, alcohol and lots and lots of sex. For Gerry at least, two out of these three vices had already been satisfied. Instead of heading for the bright lights and super clubs on the west end of the resort, they instead settled for a conventional Irish holiday pub that sat one hundred yards from where their hotel was. From two o'clock they drank as much Guinness and Irish whiskey as they possibly could. Gerry, whose eagerness for casual sex bordered on the depraved, wasted no time in getting flirtatiously acquainted with a group of girls from Newcastle on a hen week. Eddie had the indignity of waiting for Gerry as he went round the back of the pub with one of the girls, a hideously fat monstrosity called Jane. When Eddie went to fetch his friend, he caught a glimpse of the pair in their unique love-making technique, which involved Jane lying flat on her back while she and Gerry took turns in holding up her repulsive stretch-marked stomach as Gerry gamely thrust himself inside her.

Once they had finished their repulsive act of unity, an ashen-faced Gerry re-emerged from behind the pub displaying a look of abject terror. Jane, the leading lady of this romantic tryst, seemed less disturbed by what had happened. Once she finished doing what Eddie ventured was the longest piss he ever saw anyone do, beside the pub bins, in full view of the street, she pulled up her starch leggings and shouted in her thick Geordie accent, "Ah, holiday romance! Ya' canna whack it pet!" At which point Gerry violently threw up all over the brand new holiday shirt he had fondly purchased in Burtons two days before.

For Eddie the holiday was a relief to finally get away from Motherwell. It had been an emotionally fraught time. His best friend, Stubbsy, had been killed in a car accident a few weeks before. Since then he had watched his other friends react to the tragedy in their own different ways. Stevie – whom Eddie had regarded for a long time as more of a friend-of–a-friend and, although he liked him, wasn't as close to him as Stubbsy had been – had initially disappeared off the face of the Earth. He had heard a rumour that he had flown out to see his dad in Australia. This was dispelled, however, when Stevie walked into the Tavern where Eddie and Gerry were enjoying a few drinks with some of Gerry's mates from work. Although, when he thought about it now, 'enjoying' probably wasn't the right word, as he spent the full evening listening to Gerry and his colleagues telling stories from work about events he never encountered involving people he didn't know.

Stevie had come towards their table and awkwardly sat down next to them, offering up nothing more than a timid "Awrite?" Eddie thought this was strange. Although Stevie didn't usually say much, Stubbsy having done pretty much all the speaking on behalf of all of them, Stevie had always looked cool and composed, no matter what company or situation he found himself in. Now though, he seemed almost broken. His head was bowed and he was staring into space for long periods. What he also found weird was Gerry's reaction to Stevie's arrival. He practically ignored him initially and Eddie caught him on more than one occasion quietly berating him to his work friends. Thankfully, Stevie was oblivious to this at first. However, later, when they had been drinking solidly for about four hours, Gerry began making snide drunken remarks in Stevie's direction. Eventually, once Stevie had cottoned onto the fact that he was being made fun of, he spoke up.

"Gerry have you got a problem with me?" he said in a manner that Eddie felt was deliberately non-confrontational.

Gerry stared over and sneered.

"Problem? Fuckin problem, ya cunt? Only wan guy wi a problem sittin at this fuckin table mate," Gerry said, his manner the complete opposite of the one deployed by Stevie.

"And who would that be, Gerry?" Stevie said, trying not to be drawn by Gerry's antagonistic stance.

"You're a prick, mate" Gerry said. "You always huv been. Yer jist lucky the big man stood up for ye, cause if ay didnae ah wid quite happily have smashed that smug face ay yours tae a pulp bah noo. Well, big Stubbsy's no here tae protect ye, so ah suggest ye fuck off or we'll fuckin' make ye fuck off," Gerry said pointing to his friends who were lapping up his impromptu show of bravado.

Stevie, who would normally have laughed off Gerry's pathetic hard man attempt, instead looked at Eddie like a frightened kid who was pleading for help when he was at the mercy of the school bully. Eddie thought about telling Gerry to piss off and leave Stevie alone, but as was always the case when it came to him and Gerry, he said nothing and allowed Gerry a self-conceived moment of glory. Eddie knew that Gerry's hatred of Stevie wasn't because of how he felt about him personally, but of how he felt about a girl, and how that girl felt about Stevie.

Jess Richmond was a conventionally pretty blonde hairdresser who worked in the Halo Salon on Windmill Hill Street. Gerry first met her when he was fifteen and was on a mission to sort out a tricky hair situation. Two weeks previously, he had applied what he thought was rather stylish blond dye to his hair. This was a somewhat daring departure for the normally conventional, four-at-the-top three-at-the-back, Gerry Conner. Despite this, the DIY attempt at first seemed to have turned out well and for two weeks Gerry revelled in his snazzy new hairdo and the attention that came with it. That was until Glasgow Rangers unveiled their brand new summer signing. England international Paul Gascoigne was paraded to the Scottish Press sporting a garish dyed blond hairdo, remarkably similar to Gerry's, who was known as a Celtic diehard. When he went to school that morning he was mercilessly teased to the point where he decided to go straight down to the hairdressers and have his hair shaved into the wood. It was there he met Jess. She had just begun a hairstyling apprenticeship and did nothing more than make the tea and sweep the discarded hair when Gerry first met her.

This was the beginning of a fruitless period of devotion on Gerry's part. For the next two years he would religiously head for the Halo salon for his monthly haircut, each time trying and failing to muster up enough courage to ask Jess out. Then one night when Gerry was drinking in the Electric Bar with Eddie, Stubbs and Stevie, Jess came in with some friends from the salon. For Gerry, this was the chance he had been waiting for. At last he had her in a social setting away from the shampoo, clippers and inane hairdresser chat. His elation was intensified when she spotted him and waved him over enthusiastically. Egged on by his friends Gerry finally mustered up the courage to go and speak to her. As he approached her table Jess broke into a big toothy smile, which Gerry took as a good sign.

"Hiya Gerry, how's it goin'?" Jess said shifting over, allowing Gerry to sit down in their company.

"Aye awrite, just oot for a few jars wi some mates," Gerry said, pointing over towards the table where Eddie, Stubbsy and Stevie were sitting. This sent Jess's friends into fits of giggles.

"Shut it, yous!" Jess hissed, looking slightly flustered and drew them some daggered looks. Despite being relatively inexperienced with the opposite sex, Gerry interpreted Jess's blushes as a good sign and began to relax in her company. After an hour or so drinking, Gerry became frustrated with his lack of progress and started to become anxious. He had waited so long to ask Jess out that he didn't want to pass up this golden opportunity when she was in his grasp. Just as he was sizing up the best way of getting Jess on her own and ask her out, she suddenly grabbed him by the hand and began to usher him to the foyer of the pub.

"Quick, in here," Jess said trying not to make their getaway too obvious to her friends. Gerry felt his stomach flip. This was it, he thought. He didn't even have to ask her out, *she* was going to be doing it for him!

"Gerry, am really glad ah bumped into you tonight," Jess said eagerly. Gerry's mouth was completely dry and he could feel his pulse rate soar. The girl from the hairdressers whom he had lusted after for so long was actually going to ask him out.

"This is really embarrassing, ah've actually wanted to ask you this for ages now but every time you came in ah just felt stupid and couldn't do it," Jess muttered, taking a healthy swig of her long vodka.

"Eh Jess, it's fine, man, you can ask me anything, anything you like," Gerry said as he leaned against the pub inner interior, buoyed by a new sense of confidence.

"Ah don't know how to say this actually," Jess said, peering over Gerry's shoulder into the bar area. "Well, you know your friend, Stevie?"

"Aye," Gerry said, suddenly confused.

"Is he single?" Jess asked shyly.

"Is he? Why, whit dae ye mean?" Gerry spluttered.

"Well, ah know it's daft and ah know he could have any girl he wants, but, God Gerry, ah've pure fancied him since ah was like twelve and when ah saw you sitting with him tonight ah just thought "Wow, this is it, ah just *need* to ask him or will like pure die!" Jess trilled, not coming up for air.

"Eh ahm no sure, Jess, ah'll, eh ask for yee if you want?" Gerry said as he felt the wind suck straight out his stomach.

"Oh Gerry you are a total sweetheart, a pure gem, by the way. Here this is my mum's number if he wants it, he probably won't but if ay does tell him to phone me after six, ah know ay won't, but aw this pure mental, ah cannae believe it, oh Gerry you jist the best, a total wee sweetheart, by the way!" Jess's jabbering tones went through Gerry's psyche as he tried to come to terms with what had just happened. Dejected, he trudged back to the seat were his friends were sitting.

"How did ye get on wi the wee hing?" Stubbsy asked, nudging him violently in the ribs.

"Ach, no really for me, nice lassie in that but no really my cup ah tea no," Gerry said with as much enthusiasm as he could muster.

"Aye, right, ya cunt, ye were right over there like a whippet oot ay trap four up the Wishy dugs," Stubbsy laughed. At this point, Stevie came back from the bar with some drinks.

"Na man, actually she said she's intae Stevie, wants me ay give ye her number mate," Gerry said fairly, even though the words felt like sharpened razor blades as they came out his mouth.

Stevie, who had been distracted by a local guitar band that was setting up in the corner, looked round towards Jess's table and said casually, "What, the wee dumpy wan wi the blonde hair? Na, yer awrite, mate," and continued watching the band.

At the time, Eddie felt that Stevie had no intention of upsetting Gerry and, had he known how much Jess meant to him, he would never have said anything derogatory. Gerry though, was furious. All he could see in Stevie now was a smartarse rich kid from Dalziel High who thought he was better than everyone else, an opinion that over the years grew and festered.

"Get yer trunks oan them, ma sun, cannae be sittin around the apartment then, ya cunt!" Gerry commanded.

"Eh aye. It's just, ah burn like bacon an' ah've got special sun cream there an ah need help pittin it oan ma back," Eddie said, blushing crimson red.

"Well, there nabeday else here, so ah'll need tae dae it. Don't you be hittin' a hard wan noo, ya wee buftie," Gerry laughed.

"Fuck off, ya prick, ahm no ah –" Eddie shouted.

"Aye, awrite, ya daftie, ahm only windin ye up... See, in sayin' that though..." Gerry said cautiously.

"Sayin whit, Gerry, whit ye fuckin' oan aboot?" Eddie said angrily.

"Well, Eddie, it's jist, we're on hoaliday an' that, and maybe..."

"Maybe whit, Gerry, maybe whit?" Eddie snapped.

"Awrite awrite, calm doon Eddie. Look mate, it's just, you know you've no had much action in yer time, wi the wummin in that ye know?" Gerry said tactfully.

"Ah huv, whit about that..."

"Welsh lassie in Cornwall, ah know, ah know," Gerry intercepted, shaking his head sceptically. "Ahm just thinkin', we're oan holiday, fresh start, get yersel oot there. Ah mean that bint ah shagged last night, she was nae Katherine Moss," he winced at the memory of last night's shenanigans as it pricked itself back into his mind, "the complete opposite actually, but that's how it's done, ah've broke ma duck, ah can relax noo, an that's whit you should be dain."

"Aye, awrite, jist stop going oan aboot it," Eddie said, hoping that would be the last word on the matter.

After enjoying a few drinks at the pool, Eddie and Gerry reluctantly left and made their way back up to the apartment to change into their evening wear. An hour or so earlier, Gerry had managed to buy some ecstasy from the young Spanish guy who worked at the pool bar. Tonight they had decided to sample Ibiza's famous nightlife in all its glory. Gerry paced around the room, excited at the prospect of their first real night on holiday and the endless possibilities it presented. Eddie was feeling more relaxed, even though the back of his neck was burnt; even the factor fifty couldn't prevent him being cooked. The cold continental lagers he had drunk by the pool had put him in a positive frame of mind to the point where he was no longer dreading the potential drug-fuelled hijinks.

The first venue the Motherwell duo ventured into was the rather obvious Scottish bar, The Highlander. Although Gerry was always sceptical of any pub that didn't have some kind of Irish connection, he was pleasantly surprised at this pub's relaxed atmosphere. It had all the hallmarks of a Scottish holiday pub, but without the beery, rugby-playing kilt crews that usually made these places their home for the duration of their stay.

"Guinness again, Gerry?" Eddie asked pointing to the bar.

"Aye an git us a half in tae," Gerry said scanning the bar for female talent. Eddie bought the drinks and they slowly but surely felt themselves enter into a blissful state of inebriation.

By the time they'd necked four more pints and the same amount of shots, they both felt relaxed and ready to move on and kick the night up a gear. Even through his progressively drunk state, Gerry carefully fingered the little bag containing the four ecstasy tabs inside. He was acutely aware that they were the source of tonight's action and to go to one of the super clubs without them would be disastrous.

"Fuckin eckied the night then, ya cunt, eh?" Gerry said excitedly.

"Eh aye, think ah'll just take the wan though," Eddie said, disappointed that a perfectly good night on the alcohol would soon be ruined by ecstasy, a drug that he found irritating and false.

"Nae bother ma son, aw the mair for me," Gerry laughed.

They drank up and made to leave for Pasha, the most popular night club on the island. Just as they were heading for the door they noticed a crowd of girls coming in. As they drew closer Gerry's face dropped as he realised who it was.

"Wor aright there, pet?" Jane screamed as she smacked a generous kiss, which she tried to manoeuvre into a full-on snog onto Gerry's lips.

"Ha ha, he awrite, Jane? Whit's happenin?" Gerry said nervously, as he unwillingly remembered where her mouth had been the previous night.

"We're gan clubbin, well me and me best mate Lynne are anyway, headin over to that Pasha. In fact, Gerry that's what a was wantin ta talk to ya aboot," she said conspiratorially.

"Aye, whit's that then?" Gerry asked, dreading the answer.

"Well, ye no yer mate over there?" Jane asked pointing towards Eddie, who had tactfully began playing the fruit machine.

"Aye, what aboot im?" Gerry asked suddenly intrigued.

"Well me mate, Lynne, right, she's just gan through a nasty divorce and well she's come over here to take her mind off things, ya know. And she fancies your mate. You think he would be interested? We could double date!" Gerry, though appalled at the thought of going anywhere near Jane again, was delighted that his friend was at last in line for some female attention, with a girl who Gerry had to concede wasn't at all bad looking.

"Ok, sounds like a plan. We're heading over to Pasha now, we'll get you in there ok?" Gerry said giving her a matey thumbs up that he hoped exuded no sexual connotation whatsoever.

"Ohh, a canna wait, ya dirty bugger!" Jane said salaciously, cheekily pinching Gerry on the bum.

Once they had patiently waited in the lengthy queue for the nightclub, Gerry and Eddie were allowed into the club by the surprisingly relaxed bouncers and headed straight to the bar area, where, after asking for two San Miguel beers, were horrified when the black girl behind the bar with the Birmingham accent charged them twenty-two euros.

"Fuckin dear in here. Eddie, ma son, fuckin quicker we get these sweeties doon ar necks the better," Gerry said taking a sip of his beer, expecting it to taste like some magical golden nectar, given the amount they had paid for them. Unfortunately the beer was, if anything, of poorer quality than what they had been drinking in the pub earlier.

Eddie, who didn't have much experience of nightclubs, was instantly taken aback by the exotic guild he had entered. Back home he would normally head home when everyone else went out after the pub. He hated nightclubs. He always found them dark, desperate places where people were dead set on sleazy sex, violence or both. He hated how people would be in such open friendly spirits before twelve, yet became, after midnight, vampires of the night hell-bent on descending into some base carnal acts. Here though, in this brightly coloured parlour of music and vibrancy, he didn't feel anxious or intimidated by the scenes that were playing out in front of him. These weird and wonderful people, who all seemed to be feeding off a collective rhythmic energy, seemed less concerned with personal gratification and more about feeding into the vibe, a vibe he had never felt before.

"Fuckin hell Gerry, look at this place," Eddie gasped as he tried to take in the sights that were unravelling before him.

"Fuckin awrite, Eddie boy, ay? Here take this," Gerry instructed, handing him a little white pill with a Mitsubishi car logo stamped on it .Eddie was so taken by the multi coloured surroundings he took the pill without any hint of hesitation. The pair began to explore the dark and revealing corners of the nightclub where people of all different shapes and sizes danced, pouted and posed to the uplifting sounds emanating from the gigantic sound system. As they went to the bar, to get what they hoped would be more reasonably priced bottles of water, they were met by the familiar sight of Jane and her friend Lynne, who were sharing a generous fish bowl full of a thick, orange cocktail and seemed to be enjoying it very much.

"Awrite, Gerry, lad, an you must be Eddie, this is me mate Lynne," Jane shouted over the throbbing bass that seemed to be the essence of every tune that the DJ played.

"Eh awrite, Jane, how ye doing Lynne? Eh aye, this is ma mate Eddie. Ye's huvin a gid yin?" Gerry asked.

He was interrupted however when a wild-eyed Eddie, pushed past him and grabbed Lynne by the hand.

"DAAAAANCE!!!!!" he shouted and dragged a bewildered but more than willing Lynne onto the flashing laser pit that was the main dance floor. Eddie had never felt anything like it. He had taken ecstasy once before, but it only made him edgy and paranoid. He remembered Stubbsy telling him that it was a bad tablet and that the next time he tried it he would love it. Eddie's racing mind thought back to that night. My God, Eddie thought, he was right. It started with a weird twitch in his arm. Then he felt a hot sweat trickling down his back. His jaws clenched together and an uncontrollable smile formed on his face, as the pill began to pulsate through his system and take his breath away.

"Whaooo this is ah, ah itsfuckinnnamazin," Eddie said breathlessly. Lynne gave him thumbs up as she bobbed her head rhythmically from side to side. Eddie thought Lynne was beautiful, her large brown eyes, that at first looked too big for her face, now had a wondrous quality too them. Eddie, who never was one for dancing, was now feeling the music in his every fibre. Lynne was feeling Eddie's energy and began gyrating up close to him, hoping to entice him sexually.

Unfortunately for her, the ecstasy had given Eddie a life-affirming insight into who he truly was. He had fought it all his life, ever since he was eleven years old when he noticed that he was having bizarre feelings for the Chinese boy who stayed round the corner from him. He thought about the time in Stubbsy's bedroom when they watched one of his older brother's porn films. They both had pillows over there nether regions to hide their fully erect penises, although at the time Eddie was more turned on by the blond German guy with the bushy moustache, than the two scantily-clad black police women who were taking turns in sucking his considerable member.

Eddie was gay. He had always known it. But the gay lifestyle appalled him. He briefly entertained the notion of going to one of the many gay haunts in Glasgow, but he just couldn't bear the campness; it was the campness he couldn't stand. Now though, the ecstasy was liberating his emotions to the point he wanted to shout it out loud; he was coming out and wanted the world to know.

"LYNNE HONEY, YAR PURE WELL TIDY AN AH FUCKIN PURE LOVE YE, BIT IT CAN NEVER HAPPEN, ME AN YOU, YOU'RE NOT THE ONE FOR ME..." Eddie shouted into Lynne's ear.

Lynne couldn't make out a word Eddie had said, but took his mouth moving closer to her ear as a gesture of intimacy. She instinctively turned round and tried to kiss Eddie. Eddie felt Lynne's warm mouth and tongue slobber over his. After a few desperate seconds, he managed to prise himself from her.

"Naw Lynne, ye don't, ye just don't understand, it's me, ye see, am, am fuckin..." Eddie broke away and headed straight towards a small skinny guy who was camply dancing by himself, occasionally trying to integrate himself with any guy who happened to be near him. Eddie walked straight towards him, grabbed his waist and flipped him round. He then did something he had thought about doing all his life, but had never had the courage to act out. He kissed the stranger in full view of everyone then, when he was done, walked calmly out of the nightclub, leaving a stunned Lynne on her own on the dance floor.

Eddie walked in a haze across the bustling street, not quite sure where he wanted to go. The ecstasy rush from before was beginning to dissipate and he needed something to bring him back up. He thought about going back into the club to find Gerry and hoped he hadn't taken all the pills already himself. He quickly vetoed this idea, sure as he was that Lynne had probably gone back into the club and intentionally 'outed' him to Jane and his friend. He needed a drink. He spotted a quiet pre-club type bar called Plastik. When he entered, the cool air purring out from the air conditioning was a refreshing change from the hot muggy ambience of the street outside. All around him were fantastic looking woman and men. The girls were tanned and fit and the men were the most unconventional he had ever seen; some were even wearing make-up that fell just below full-on tranny, but was exotic enough to make them stand out from the crowd. Eddie went to the bar and asked for a beer. His head was fuzzy and as he fished money from his pocket he felt as though he was moving in slow motion.

"Five euros please, mate," the barman said.

Through his druggy haze Eddie looked up to acknowledge him. He was ruggedly good looking and had a familiar Scottish accent. His face was recognisable, but Eddie couldn't quite work out where from. He was tanned and muscular and his hair was shaven almost to the bone. When he smiled he flashed an amazing set of white teeth. He had perfect designer stubble, interrupted by two fresh looking slash marks on each side of his face that, although they looked like they were the result of an extreme bout of violence, somehow it made him look even more attractive to the point Eddie felt himself flushing when he began to speak.

"Scottish, aye?" he said, beaming a winning smile at Eddie.

"Eh aye, ahm fae, eh Motherwell," Eddie stuttered.

"Aye? I'm from Wishaw originally. I live out here now though," the barman said proudly.

"Fuckin weird, mate, as soon as ah saw you, ah recognised you. Dae ye drink in the Tavern?" Eddie inquired.

"No, I didn't socialise much in Motherwell. In fact, I never really socialised anywhere back home. If you ever done your shopping in Safeway up in Wishaw, that's where you probably know me, I used to spend my life up there. I'm Alistair by the way."

"Aye, sound, ahm Eddie," he said offering his sweaty hand. "You'll need to forgive me mate, ah took an E earlier and it's startin to wear off."

"Tut tut, a Motherwell man letting the side down by dabbling in illicit substances, I don't know..." Alastair teased.

"Naw, naw, ah don't usually take..."

"I'm winding ye up, mate," Alastair laughed. "Look, why don't you go in there and take a wee snort of this?" he suggested, pointing to the toilets and producing a healthy-sized wrap of cocaine.

Although back home this was another drug Eddie wasn't used to dabbling in, he grabbed it instinctively, took it into a cubicle in the toilet and snorted a large, medicinal line. The drug had an instant effect. Whereas before the ecstasy filled him with love and happiness, now the coke had charged him with a cocksure confidence that was completely out of character. When he returned to the bar, it was empty; only Alastair remained. He noticed that he had a fresh bottle of beer and shot waiting for him. He wasn't sure if it was the drink, the drugs or the overall liberation of the night, but as Eddie watched Alastair lift the bar stools and put them on the table, he felt an electric sexual urge wash all over him.

"For me?" Eddie asked, a hint of flirtation in his voice. Alistair, who was now pouring himself a drink picked up on the vibe and sat as close to Eddie as he possibly could.

"So, Eddie boy, where are your friends, or are you all alone?" he asked staring directly into Eddie's eyes.

"Naw man, ahm wi ma mate, he's still in the club. Although to be honest ah think our friendship ended the night," Eddie said, his mouth hoarse with anticipation.

"Oh really and why is that?" Alistair asked.

"Well, he has probably found out by now that ahm, as he would put it, a 'buftie'. To be honest wi ye though, ah couldnae give a fuck," Eddie said, matching Alastair's stare.

"You'll need somewhere to stay then?" Alastair teased.

"Eh aye, ah will," Eddie said nervously.

Alistair, picking up on Eddie's nervousness put his hand on his knee and said, "You can crash at mine, I've only the one bed though," and with this, he leant over and planted a hot, anticipated kiss on Eddie's lips. Once they both came up for air, they went out, flagged a taxi, went back to Alistair's flat and had the most robust sex that either of them had ever encountered.

"So how did you end up here then?" Eddie asked, lying back on Alistair's double bed, feeling both scared and excited about what had just taken place.

"Well about six months ago I was on the receiving end of a serious beating, hence the Edward Scissorhands look," Alistair said, rubbing the left-sided scar on his face. "It was a traumatic time, but strangely, it acted as a kind of epiphany. It made me realise that I was living a lie, that I was trying to be someone I wasn't. I ended my marriage that night. Went back to stay with my parents for a while, before I met a guy in Delmonica's, you know the gay place in town?"

"Eh aye," Eddie said even though he had never heard of it. Suddenly he wanted Alistair to think he was a major face in the Glasgow gay scene, an aspiration that only a couple of hours ago would have been ridiculous.

"Well he knew a guy who owned a few bars out here and was looking for someone with managerial experience to run them. And even though I had never worked in a pub before, I jumped at the chance. Been out here eight weeks now, am loving it to be honest," Alistair said earnestly.

"So what was your wife like then?" Eddie softly inquired.

Alistair went silent for a moment. He gulped, trying not to let the pain of his wife's memory engulf him. "She is the most wonderful woman I have ever met. She still phones me now and again, always wanting to know I'm ok," Alistair said, his voice suddenly cracking with emotion. "I love her, love her more than I will ever love anyone. It's my biggest regret that I couldn't be the one for her," he said, wiping a tear from his eye. "I honestly pray every single day that she meets someone special, a guy who's as smart and individualistic as her, someone who will make her feel as special as I know she is."

Alistair was sobbing lightly now. He knew he had done the right thing walking away from his marriage, but the possibility that he had hurt Marie in any way broke his heart.

"Ahm sure she will, mate," Eddie said taking Alistair by the hand and squeezing it softly. "Alastair, how did you know, ah mean you were married in that, but did you always know you were gay?" Eddie asked, sitting himself upright on the bed.

"Didn't realise until a few months back," Alistair said matter-of-factly.

"Aye, fuck me, so how did you know then, what happened?" Eddie asked suddenly intrigued.

"Well, after Marie and I split, I started seeing this young girl Tracy from work. She was this plain wee thing who, looking back now, was rather boyish looking. She was very submissive and would let me do pretty much anything to her. After a while we realised that I performed best when we had sex... eh you know?" Alastair winced embarrassingly.

"No, ah don't," Eddie said puzzled.

"Well, sex the way we just did it," Alistair said, trying not to sound too puritanical. "It came to a head one night when Tracy was acting out a... erm, particular fantasy of mine."

"OH AYE, DO TELL!" Eddie roared.

"It's too embarrassing, I don't want to say," Alastair replied sheepishly.

"Oh no, you said it now, you have to tell me!" Eddie demanded.

"Ok, ok. Well, I used to get her to dress up as a nineteen-eighties Celtic supporter," Alistair said evenly.

"What... what do you mean?" Eddie was incredulous.

"I managed to get hold of a Celtic top from that time, a pair of Adidas Samba and an old pair of Wrangler jeans," Alastair said trying to keep a straight face.

"And that did it for you?" Eddie inquired.

"Oh yeah, and she was great. She would drink a half-bottle of Buckfast before it and sing Celtic songs while I happily pumped her up the arse." At this they both collapsed into a heap of uncontrollable laughter. "She just said to me one, night, 'Alistair, you're gay aren't you?' It kind of sunk in then."

Once the hysterics had finally finished, they lay peacefully in each other's arms, the silence only being punctuated by a speeding vehicle from outside.

"What you going to do with the rest of the holiday then?" Alistair asked.

"Dunno, Gerry won't want to speak to me and, to be honest, ah couldn't care less. Ah see him for what he is now, a pathetic wanker who will never be happy within himself," Eddie forcibly admitted.

"Well, you can always stay here. I can show you the sights," Alistair offered with a hint of mischief in his tone.

"Ah thought you'd never ask mate," Eddie said, suddenly lifting his leg over and straddling Alistair. He took his head in his hands and delicately stroked it. "By the way, mister," he whispered, "ah have the new Celtic strip in my suitcase, top, shorts and socks."

Alistair laughed, but couldn't help a fizz of excitement bolt through him. He didn't really know this guy, or where it was going, but, for now, the thought of him in green and white stripes was too good to turn down. He felt his testicles recoil into the sac and his cock pulse into a throbbing erection. It truly was a grand old team to play for!

DIARY ENTRY 46

2002 September

SUNDAY

WHEN THE SUN SHINES IN NEW YORK, EVERYONE SEEMS TO FEEL LIKE THEY HAVE BEEN BLESSED by God and to repay him, they smile and laugh, flirt and swoon with friends and strangers alike. It one of the many things that reminds me of Scotland.

Amie has settled in fine. I got a call from the nursery, or kindergarten as they call it out here. She had apparently kicked a little boy who was teasing her because she doesn't have a "real mommy". I try to tell her that she can say I am her real mommy, but she never listens.

"No, Clare, you're my pretend mummy," she will say. I can't tell you how that makes me feel inside.

I sometimes think, did I kill her "real mommy" or was it circumstances? Was it situational? One thing I do know, I have to stop the negative thoughts.

"Ye gatta get outta that negative place," Dianne, my therapist constantly tells me.

Going out with Dan tonight. First date. We got to know each other on MySpace. His band, The Prevention, ("Yeah, we're, like, better than The Cure!") had some songs on there and I stumbled across them. They're actually really good. Quite similar to The Strokes, The Walkman and a load of other New York garage bands doing the rounds at the moment. We met properly a few weeks ago. I was still nervous about leaving Amie with a sitter, so he came round for coffee one afternoon. He's been round for drinks a few nights too and last week, well, he stayed the night.

I've started working for a care centre, looking after kids whose mothers are hooked on drugs. This is one part of New York life that is not in any way glamorous.

The relationship I've built with Amie has restored my faith in the maternal instinct that most people take for granted. Dianne insists this is to do with what happened with Jack (we both agreed on our first session not to call him Dad) and, in particular, my mother's indifference to it. She thinks I have to confront her about what happened that night. She has no idea that it's far too late for that now.

I think about my mum sometimes. Does she miss me? She knows, like Jack, that I am still alive. She has, no doubt, decided to play along and hope that I never return. Does she love me? I don't particularly care. When I made love to Dan the other night it felt like the first time I did ANYTHING. It felt... pulsating. It wasn't all lovey-dovey, but it felt good. I had tried sex before, just to make sure what happened with my dad didn't affect me in later life. This time, however, it was for the right reasons. For the first time I am genuinely attracted to somebody.

So in my new life, Dan is helping me forget my father. Dianne and Amie are helping me move on from my feelings towards my mum. Which leaves just one person, one Scottish ghost. I can't though; I just can't cope with him in my mind. I lie at night and worry that I abandoned him like all the rest. And the reason I do that is because I did. But I have to move on.

Steven Costello. I am sorry.

CHAPTER 22

LETTERS FROM LISA

Dear Stevie,

I'm writing this letter to you from my new home in Berlin. I moved here last month with Paul, my real dad. It's really strange. Even in a letter I don't know what to say to you. I often think about the last year and wonder if there were things I would change. I can't tell you the heartache it caused me keeping Clare's secret from you all that time. There were a few occasions when I nearly told you, such was the weight of the secret I was carrying, but, at the end of the day, I had made a promise and believed I was doing the right thing.

I never told you what happened the night Stubbs died. As you were probably aware, our surface hatred of each other concealed a deep affection that we both tried hard to deny. However, that night we opened ourselves up and realised we had found the one thing we wanted more than anything. Stevie, I don't think I will ever get over losing him, I still think about him every day. I don't want to lecture you Stevie, I know I'm in no position to do so, but at his funeral you showed no emotion. I don't know why you're like this, or what it is you are trying to hide from, but I hope that one day you can find some way of resolving this issue because bottling everything inside is not good for the soul.

I know I'll probably never see you again, but wish you every happiness in life,

Your friend,

Lisa.

CHAPTER 23

THAT NIGHT WE MET ON ORBISTON STREET

Sometimes, when I'm on my own, lying here in bed, I try to consider how I ended up here. Not this place, the flat, physically, but in this position, this state of mind. This time last year I was going out with Clare, Lisa and I were about start our second year in our new flat and Stubbsy, Eddie and Gerry were, well, they were just there. Now though, one by one, they have all gone and I don't know why.

I haven't spoken to anybody in two weeks. I have arranged to go see Aunt May and Uncle John, whom I stayed with when my dad went to Australia. I don't particularly want to see them, but I feel I should, to get out of this flat if anything. The place needs some attention, but I don't have the energy to clean up. I wake in the morning and lie here, holding onto my pillow; holding on like I am about fall down somewhere. I haven't been to work for nearly six weeks now. I asked for some compassionate leave after Stubbsy's funeral. They said I could have a fortnight, but no more. I didn't bother going back. Never even phoned. I would have if Alastair had still been there. He wasn't though, he hasn't returned since after *that* night.

I have since heard a crazy rumour that he handed his notice in and fled the country. I can only hope it's true and that he and his wife are living a life somewhere that's better than anything Pishy Wishy can offer. It's strange how Clare, Alastair and Lisa, the three people I knew who, collectively, had the most grounded of ambitions, have done what I always wanted to do; they have managed to get out of Motherwell. They are living the life I have always dreamed of, and I can't quite work out how it happened.

I always believed that there was a thin line between boredom and loneliness. When you're on your own for considerable amounts of time, it's sometimes hard to know the difference. What I mean by this is that a man will happily go weeks without having any real company, but not feel particularly down about it, and the real reason he goes to the pub every night is not to drown away the sorrowful situation he finds himself in, but merely to combat the boredom. On the other hand a man can be surrounded by people who are in his life constantly, close family and friends for instance, but if the one person he wants to be with the most isn't there he will feel incredibly lonely.

My problem is that I'm lonely, but not for the people who have left me. I've been thinking about my dad a lot recently. Our relationship was never as good as it should have been and I'm willing to admit that I could've been a more loving son. Despite this, he is the only living person who has never let me down. Okay, he could have been more emotionally available, but at least he has never tried to be something to me that he wasn't. He has continued to send over money, he has always been in touch at important times, birthdays and Christmas and so forth, and has always made me feel that I could go and live with him at any time. I miss him. I miss him because he is my dad and I love him and at the moment he's all I have. I want to start again with him, build a new relationship and hold onto the only family I have left.

My Aunt May is my dad's sister. We get on fine I suppose, but of late she and I have not been in touch as much as we should. Her husband, John, is a tall quiet man who rarely says much. I always got the impression that he resented the troubles I brought on his family, from my mum leaving to me staying with them for a time. He never said as much, it wasn't his style, but he always made it clear to me that he didn't want me around.

To be fair, these days he wasn't the only one. I was given a rather public insight into how Gerry felt about me a few weeks back in the Railway Tavern. To be honest, I had never seen eye to eye with him and, had it not been for his friendship with Stubbsy, I would never have had any contact with him. I remembered that him and wee Eddie were due to go for a week's holiday in Ibiza, so I popped into the Tavern to wish them all the best. What transpired was a rather pathetic attempt by Gerry to make fun and intimidate me. It was embarrassing, but the truth is if I never see Gerry again it would make no difference to me. The only disappointment was Eddie's reaction. I liked Eddie, still do if I am honest, but I thought he might have stepped in when Gerry was acting like such a dick, but he didn't. He seemed to be more interested in looking at his shoes than standing up to his pal. However, if the last few months have taught me anything, it's not to expect too much from those around you. I've tried, for my own sanity more than anything, to make sense of Lisa and Clare's betrayal. I can understand, in a strange way, why they elaborately lied to me, but what they didn't do when they hatched their ornate plan was to think of how it would affect me. Now I know that's sounds selfish, but I can't help it. It seemed they made sure everyone was catered for except me and it feels like it's me who has lost the most.

Two significant things have happened to me over the last couple of months. Firstly, Stubbsy's death. I can't begin to quantify just how large a hole his passing has left in my life. I think about him every day and still can't believe he's gone. The other occurrence was the revelation that Jack Murray, who was my political hero and who became like a second father to me, may have raped his own daughter, my ex-girlfriend. Now, I don't have any concrete proof of this, I only have Lisa's testament, but something that happened recently makes me think that he did abuse his daughter. At the last meeting I had with his impact team, I couldn't look Jack in the eye, to the point where he twice asked me if I was ok. When I finally did, it was when I deliberately brought up a measure that had been discussed in Parliament earlier that year: where predatory paedophiles, i.e. those who prey on children they know, should be dealt with more severely than opportunist abusers. My gaze burned right through Jack and he knew something wasn't right. Jack is a very smart man and he obviously sensed that I was now privy to some information that would destroy him. A week later I received an e-mail from the impact team's chief-coordinator, Jeff Pearson, telling me that although my efforts over the last two years were greatly appreciated, they were no longer required.

My feeling towards Jack is a toxic mix of hatred and disgust. I know that Clare probably wanted to run away and start a new life and hope she never had to think about the night her own father raped her. However, I feel that the moment when she decided to keep me out the loop with her plan, she forfeited any say in how I would deal with it, were I to ever find out. I have a plan of my own. Next year the Scottish Parliament will dissolve and a new election will be called. This promises to be one of the tightest contests yet, with a revived SNP gaining serious ground on Labour. I will, at the right moment, go on record and state that the reason Jack's daughter committed suicide was because her father raped her when she was a teenager. The fallout will be massive; the press may or may not believe my story, but it will finish Jack and frankly, I don't care.

My Aunt May lives in an old sturdy looking council house in the guts of North Motherwell. When I arrive, I can immediately feel there's a tense atmosphere. Instead of Uncle John sitting on his chair watching the racing and Aunt May cooking, baking or both, they are nervously sitting in the kitchen as if they have been waiting for me to arrive and are about to engage in a rehearsed speech.

"Sit doon, son," Uncle John says.

"Is everything ok? Aunt May, what's the matter?" My aunt looks away and begins to cry softly. This is weird.

"Liston son, yer aunt... well, May and ah think it's best you don't come round here anymore. Now we have our reasons, but ah don't see any point in going over them now. We just think its best you get on with your life without us."

I look for a minute to see if they are joking, but my Aunt May's efforts not to look in my direction tell me that this isn't a joke.

"With all due respect, John, Aunt May is practically the only family ah have, so if there is something ah've done to upset you both, ah'd like you tell me what it is."

At this point my Aunt May leaps to her feet and explodes into a fit of rage, "BECAUSE YER JIST LIKE HER, THAT BLOODY MOTHER OF YOURS, YERR JUST

LIKE HER. EVERYWERE YOU GO YOU BRING MISERY,
JUST LIKE SHE DID. IF YOU ONLY KNEW WHAT
THAT WUMMIN PUT MY BROTHER THROUGH AND
WITHOUT A HINT AY REGRET, THE COLD HEARTED
BITCH"

"May, that's enough," John says trying to take May by
the arm and sit her down.

"NAW, JOHN, THIS HAS TO BE SAID. YER JUST LIKE
HER, STEVEN. AT THE FUNERAL FOR THAT PERR
WEE LASSIE YE WERE SEEING, YE NEVER EVEN
FLINCHED, NOT WAN BIT AY EMOTION. AN WEE
JEAN THAT HOUSEKEEPS FOR THE CHAPEL SAID IT
WAS THE SAME FOR YER PAL. SHE SAID SHE'D
NEVER SEEN SO MANY PEOPLE'S HERT BROKEN,
YET YOU, YOU WERE LIKE MISTER BLOODY ICE.
WELL, YE GET THAT FROM YER MOTHER AND I
DON'T WANT ANY TRACE AY THAT WUMMIN
AROUND ME OR MY FAMILY!" She sits down and
takes a gulp of her tea that she has been nursing since
I came in.

I'm totally crushed by this. I'm completely numb and
can't think what to say, "You're all ah've got Aunt
May, ah just..."

"Aw, son, c'mon, is you no supposed to be the wan wi
the brains, huv ye no worked it oot yet?" May says
evenly.

"Right, May, ah mean it, that's enough. Listen son, ah
think it's best that you go," John says nodding
towards the door.

"Ahm nae aunt ay yours, Tony isnae your father, son. No yer real one anyway. That harlot ay a mother ay yours was having an affair wi some hoodlum type, ever since she got her claws intae ma brother That's why she left, tae start a new life wi him. Left ma brother tae pick up the pieces. We're no you family son, we never huv been and it's time ye accept it," May announces calmly.

"No, it's, he is my dad, you can't say that, please don't say that," I say as a lump in my throat threatens to overtake and envelope into a tsunami of emotion, but again I suppress it.

"Just go, Steven, please, just leave," Aunt May says as she leaves the kitchen.

I turn and walk out the back door. John comes running out after me.

"Steven, son, listen, May's upset, it's just it's for the best all this, fresh start. Listen, why ye don't phone yer old man. I think you and he need to talk."

He's talking, but I can't hear the words. It's numb. I can't hear and I can't feel. I can't feel because I can't cry. I just need to be somewhere, somewhere…

ORBISTON STREET

How did I get here, walking aimlessly through Orbiston Street? The clouds take turns in blanking out the sun, which has decided to make one last appearance before a harsh violent winter takes over and envelopes the old town. I know why I'm here. I'm here to try and feel it, feel what he felt. It begins with a bingo hall and ends in an underpass and the unspoken romances in-between. It was the most poetic thing he ever said. I remember I always wanted to ask him why it meant so much, why it held so much romantic resonance, but then, maybe by asking him, I would somehow point out that it was only a street, and the magic would disappear.

I'm sitting on a bench watching everything and nothing go by. Some serious wee neds are making a nuisance of themselves at the mouth of the underpass. They leer and holler at everyone who goes past. They spit and swear and seem to have no thought of anyone else around them. There's an old lady who looks like she wants to go through the underpass, but wisely decides against it. I watch her as she struggles up the hill to cross the busy road. Just as she reaches the top of the hill, she loses her balance and falls over. I instinctively move to help her. Then something beautiful happens. The neds at the underpass, who the old lady was so keen to avoid, are up and racing towards her. The first pair to arrive bend down to see if she is ok, another has taken his top off and is cradling the lady's head. His friend has flicked her phone up and looks to be dialling the emergency services. I sit back down and take it in. Is this what he meant? Does this place have some magical pull that brings the best out in people?

The emergency services arrive and the young team stay with the old lady until she is safely in the ambulance. It touches me, really touches me. I feel something catch the back of my throat. My life and all it's worth seems to pass before my eyes and I can't seem to breathe, and now I just... am feeling... I... I... I can't look, my head is in my hands and I can't breathe, my shoulders are shaking and my eyes are blurred and the tears, the tears are flowing down my face. I want my dad. I want Lisa and Clare, but more than anything I want him... Aw, Stubbsy, man, Stubbsy, please, please help me. I miss you, I miss you so much and I don't think I can do this without you. I am on my knees now and crying so hard that people are coming towards, trying to talk to me.

"Hey mate, aw mate whit's wrang man?" One of the young team has approached me and is trying to lift my arm. I can't move though, I just can't feel anything, but the sadness, the sadness that Stubbsy's dead.

"Hey, leave him alone!" Two student girls, probably from the college, have come to see what the fuss is. They immediately assume, as I did, that the youngster is up to no good.

"Ahm jist seein if the cunt's awrite, fir fuck sake man, try ay dae ah good turn no," the poor guy pleads. At this point a middle-aged man in a suit has crouched down and lifted my head.

"Son, are you ok? Is there someone I can phone to come and get you?" I am crying silently now, my head tucked into my chest. There is no one he can phone. There is no one.

"Ahm ok, just let me go, ah can walk."

The strangers who stopped to help begin to part and allow me to rise to my feet and I aimlessly walk down towards the bingo hall. My phone rings. I ignore it. The phone rings for a second time. It's my dad. I hesitate initially then flick my phone up.

"Hello," I say, still twitching like an infant who's just recovering from an almighty tear-soaked tantrum.

"Steven, it's your dad," he says tersely.

"Aye, awrite, Dad," I say fighting to keep my emotions in check.

"Steven, your Uncle John just phoned. He told me what happened. Are you ok?"

"Does it matter?" I counter, as another tear begins to well up in my eye.

"What do you mean 'does it matter?'" he asks, forcefully.

"Well am not yours, and like John and May said, I'm a fuckin pollution to anyone ah meet," I say, feeling sorry for myself.

"Right you, now you listen here. First off, your Aunt May is a mad old duffer and she won't know what side her mouth is on when I'm finished with her. Secondly, I couldn't care what your mother did or who she did it with. You are my son, Steven, and that is the end of it, do you hear me? I am serious, Steven."

"Aye, it's just... ah've had a time of it here, Dad, and ah miss you."

"Steven, no matter what happened with me and your mum, I brought you up. You are mine and I can't begin to tell you proud I am of you." I can hear his voice crack with emotion. "You come over as soon as you can, I'll get Mandy to organise the flights. I'll always be here for you, Steven, remember that," he says, his feelings beginning to flow from his words now.

"Thanks, Dad."

Orbiston Street is peacefully quiet. It's a familiar gentle hush that descends on the old steel town when everyone is home from work, but not quite ready to go back out again. I am remarkably placid. I remember Linda, the counsellor from the college I had seen, telling me that crying was an immensely cathartic experience and how you can usually feel a sense of punctuated ease after you've cried. I now know what she means. I am sitting on this bench wondering what and where life will take me. Suddenly, from nowhere, I hear a soft familiar voice, from someone I thought I would never see again.

"Hey Stevie," she says as she flicks her hair over her shoulders.

"Hey Marie, God, it's good to see you," I say honestly. I had always noticed her obvious beauty, but as she was my boss's wife, it was always from a wishful distance. Now I think she is possibly the most beautiful woman I have ever set eyes on.

"Stevie, are you ok, you look like you've been…"

I interrupt her before she gets a chance to point out the obvious.

"Crying? Well, that'd be because ah have. Marie, today was a lousy day, but…ach fuck it, y'know what, ahm feeling like a bad Nick Cave song. Listen, would you like to join me for a drink somewhere?" I say, pointing to the assortment of pubs on Windmill Hill Street.

"Well I've got the car, but fuck it, where you taking me, sailor boy?" she teases.

"Allow me," I say as I offer her my arm, which she naturally hooks into hers. "You know, someone once told this was the most romantic street in the world and do you know what? I think he was right."

"Mmmm, let's get the drinks in and see where the night takes us," Marie laughs.

And as we walk towards the Starka bar, I think about Stubbsy, and whether or not he can see me walk with this beautiful woman on my arm. Something he always said, something that just about summed up everything in my life, comes into my head. It doesn't matter where you are or what you do, the time or the date or the place. It is those you are with that count the most. And it's those who will count forever.

You may also enjoy:

Head Boy
By
Mark Wilson

Follow Davie Diller for seven days as he navigates his way through his turbulent life. A scheming bastard in and out of school, Diller screws, drinks, snorts, cons and kills his way through the Lanarkshire underworld and attempts to survive the attention of his local drug-lord, Hondo, who's less than impressed by Diller's growing debt and status; He's also having a busy week at school.

Praise for Head Boy:

"His Diller creation is in equal measures compulsive and repulsive." - **Ryan Bracha, author of Tomorrow's Chip Paper and Paul Carter is a Dead Man.**

"The main character pulls off the ultimate deception that even the most observant reader does not fully comprehend until the very end." – **Craig Furchtenicht, author of Dimestore Bandits.**

Printed in Great Britain
by Amazon

35968233R00170